Prairie Ostrich

Also by Tamai Kobayashi

Quixotic Erotic
Exile and the Heart

Co-authored with Mona Oikawa
All Names Spoken

TAMAI KOBAYASHI

Prairie Ostrich

a novel

Edited by Bethany Gibson.
Cover and page design by Julie Scriver.
Cover image inspired by Origami Wind, flickr.com.
Original origami ostrich designed and folded by Quentin Trollip.
Feather image by Alexandra Bereza, Veer.
Printed in Canada.
10 9 8 7 6 5 4 3 2 1

Library and Archives Canada Cataloguing in Publication

Kobayashi, Tamai, 1966-, author
Prairie ostrich / Tamai Kobayashi.

Issued in print and electronic formats.
ISBN 978-0-86492-680-7 (pbk.).—ISBN 978-0-86492-749-1 (epub)

I. Title.

PS8571.O33P73 2014   C813'.54   C2013-907294-2
C2013-907295-0

Goose Lane Editions acknowledges the generous support of the Canada Council for the Arts, the Government of Canada through the Canada Book Fund (CBF), and the Government of New Brunswick through the Department of Tourism, Heritage, and Culture.

Goose Lane Editions
500 Beaverbrook Court, Suite 330
Fredericton, New Brunswick
CANADA E3B 5X4
www.gooselane.com

To Bo Yih
with love

1974
Bittercreek, Alberta

September

Egg Murakami is eight years old and her feet are perfect. Not everyone can say that. She dangles her feet over the edge of the bed and clicks her tongue. The crisp autumn light spills over the ledge of her window, throwing shadows across the floor. Mornings are new, like a fresh sheet of paper. Mornings are new, without any mistakes. She can hear her mother in the kitchen, the metallic clatter of the kettle on the stove. Her big sister Kathy twists the tap in the bathroom, a squeak that runs through the pipes in the floors. It is almost peaceful. Nekoneko, her puppet Kitty with the homemade eye patch, stands guard on her bedside table, gazing over the smash and scatter of Lego and dinky cars strewn on the faded russet rug. Beneath her window lies the barrens of southern Alberta, the stunted grass that sweeps into the Badlands. To the right, the sagging barn with its long wire pens. Left, the stubble fields that roll to the horizon. She taps her heels together. The low groan of the barn gate rumbles through the air. The ostriches burst from their enclosure, shaggy feathers hovering above the ground, legs a blur of spindly angles, as if in flight after all. Across the pen, down the line of the fence, they run with a frantic energy—then stop, stiff, as if confronted by an immovable object. The ostriches spin, twirling, their wings spread as if to greet the day, heads held high in a dizzying, exuberant dance.

"Egg!" her sister calls from below.

Egg dashes into the bathroom and dunks her head under the sputtering tap. Pat pat pat, her hands against her head, she likes the wet sound, like her duck feet after the bath. Pat pat pat. She doesn't like the scratch of the porcupine brush or the cold droplets that snake down her back, slithering into the groove of her spine. With a shake, she plops on the edge of the bathtub and rubs her head with her favourite blue towel. She knows her hair is short for a girl but she likes it that way. As small as she is, Egg can't quite see herself in the mirror above the basin so she stretches, balancing on her toes. The key is to get the bigger picture. She knows that things have a purpose, that she must get it right.

In her socks, Egg glides down the hallway, as if on ice. She's like the Flash, so fast you can see only a blur. The Flash is almost invisible, but it is the *almost* that troubles her, the red streak of *almost* that catches the eye. Superheroes save the day. She knows they are fiction, but a part of her wants so much for them to be real, like Newton's equal and opposite forces. Egg thinks of the bumblebee bats in Kathy's *National Geographic*. Bumblebee bats, newly discovered, are the smallest mammals ever.

At the top of the landing, Egg tucks in her shirt and descends the stairs. She slips her toes into the gaps of the banister and skips over the loose boards that can give her away. The last step is tricky; she presses one foot against the wall and the other against the bottom railing. From this perch, she can see her Mama in the kitchen. Between them, the darkness of the hall, the brooding half-light of the alcove falls against the stillness of the china cabinet.

Mama is at the sink, with the flutter of her apron, her eyes turning from the window. Dust motes swirl and the scent of cinnamon fills the air. A bright and early-morning Mama.

Egg bounces on her tiptoes, an almost hello.

The bottle scrapes against the counter as her mother slides the whiskey behind the flour bin. The sound rakes down Egg's back, like the scratch of jagged nails, like the game of X Marks the Spot. Her Mama's silence is like broken glass. Egg waits. She knows that words are important, that Albert would have known what to say. Her big brother could charm a smile out of a rattlesnake and tip his cap like a cowboy movie star.

But Albert is dead dead dead and the Starlight drive-in off Highway Seven closed down. The big screen, once so towering, is now just a peeling, streak-stained wall, a crumbling blank. The rows upon rows of speakers, abandoned and ghostly, stand in patient vigil over the eruption of weeds in the cracks of the pavement. Bittercreek, rust and dust, Albert had laughed, although Egg can't remember when he had said that, or why. There are so many things she can't quite understand. When she thinks of her brother, her heart clutches up, her throat tightens.

Bye bye Albert.

At the bottom of the stairs, Egg slips into her shoes. She wiggles her toes. "Better safe than sorry," she whispers.

Kathy bristles by in her foulest morning temper. Kathy Grumpycakes Moodymug Murakami. Egg dodges, too late, too slow; her shoulder bumps the edge of the china bureau. The crystal figures tinkle and sparkle, catching a splash of light, scattering droplets to the floor. Egg freezes, and for a moment time holds, like the strike of a chime in an ancient tower.

"Mom," Kathy's big-sister voice. "Egg's got her shoes on wrong."

Flutter. There are bluebirds fading on Mama's apron.

Egg shuffles into the kitchen and slips into her chair. "I don't want to go to school," she says, but her words fall between Kathy's glare and her Mama's distraction. Invisibility is the best superpower, better than X-ray vision.

Her mother does not turn from the window. "Egg, put your shoes on right," she sighs. Her voice is worn, like pebbles in a riverbed. She reaches behind the flour bin.

Egg sinks into her stomach as Mama takes up her glass. Rapunzel had a tower with neither stairs nor doors but Egg knows the difference between fairy tales and real life. She grabs the milk but the waxy carton is slick from the cold of the fridge. Sweaty. She doesn't like the squishy feel of the box. It almost slips from her fingers, so she squeezes — too tightly. Milk erupts from the spout, splashing over her bowl, onto her shirt, to the floor.

"Oh, for Christ's sake," Kathy curses and pushes away from the table.

Egg taps her feet together.

Her mother turns and sees the mess of the milk, the bowls. "Oh Kathy, couldn't you look out for your sister for once in your life?"

Kathy narrows her eyes. "What? This is my fault?"

Mama takes two steps and wipes Egg's shirt with her apron. "It's the first day of school and first impressions..." She peers closely. "Egg, your shirt's inside out."

"Outside's dirty." Egg blinks at the apron strings, the frozen flight of wings. Bluebirds of happiness.

"Well, now the inside's dirty, sweetpea."

Kathy leans against the counter, her body sneering. "No use crying over it."

Her mother stiffens.

"Kathy. Take the breakfast tin out to your father."

"Jeez—"

"And don't you have a dress for the first day of school?"

Kathy snatches the tin from the counter. As the door slams behind her, Kathy's footsteps land heavy on the porch boards. Kathy, who broods like storm clouds, who crashes like thunder. Egg can see her sister through the window, kicking at the gravel as she makes her way to the barn. Egg turns to her Mama. She feels the sudden contraction of space, a chill in the pit of her stomach.

Her mother, smudged at the edges, is gone gone gone. Like the shadows in the drive-in on Highway Seven. Gone like Albert.

"Mama?"

Mama flinches.

"Mama?" Egg repeats, the word cracking on her tongue. She feels a roughness in her throat, like she is swallowing sand.

Her Mama blinks as if to bring the room into focus. "Your new pants," she exclaims loudly. "Sweetheart, you want school to be different from last year, don't you?"

Egg bites her lip. Was last year her fault?

"And your hair, sweetie, your hair," Mama whispers as she pushes back Egg's tangles, even as she pulls her closer.

Egg bows her head, holds the weight of her mother's hands, the clasp of her bosom. She can hear her mother's heart beating through the bluebird apron and feel her Mama's stomach, in and out with every breath, her smell of whiskey and mints kept in the kitchen drawer. Egg knows her mother is choking on the liquor but Egg is too small for this and she doesn't have the words. She waits. All of her life is waiting. Her mother's arms open from the crush of bluebirds and Egg is released into this day, this morning, like a bird that can't quite fly.

. . .

"Cumulus nimbus!" Egg screeches as she bursts outside and the screen door slaps joyfully behind her. Her arms flap as she leaps off the porch. "Cumulus nimbus!" Egg shouts, because she likes the words.

Above her the sky is a brilliant blue, the sun dazzling, in the full burst of the morning. Egg can see Kathy standing at the gates and behind her, the shadow of her father. Her father, who never leaves the ostrich barn, not anymore, not since Albert died. Dead dead dead, Egg repeats to herself. But Jesus rose, and Lazarus too. They said so, in Sunday school.

The light falls through the barred windows of the ostrich barn; colours bleed, a patina of dust. Four rectangular wire pens, the outside run for the ostriches, stretch out along the southern side of the barn, a stone's throw from the slough. The ostriches doze in their enclosure, their heads tucked under wings, a mass of feathers. Their sinewy legs look reptilian, shockingly naked beneath the heavy plumes. Egg knows the story, of how in the first year the ostriches went blind, their eyes clouded from ammonia in their urine mixing with the straw. They ran, panicked by the scent of stray dogs and coyotes, and ended up twisting in the wire fences, or snapping their legs in the prairie dog holes. It took two seasons but Papa got it right—the feed, the ammonia, the dogs fenced out and coyotes shot, the patchwork of gopher hides nailed to the old barn wall.

Egg watches closely. It is her job now. Her father and Kathy stand, as if they are in a television show with the sound turned off. Kathy, with the hook of her thumb tugging at her belt loop and Papa doing the same. Egg thinks of a push-me-pull-you from her illustrated *Doctor Dolittle*. Kathy and Papa are like that. They want things but they will never say. And so Papa goes back into the barn. Kathy is seventeen, as if she knows everything. She'd bust out of herself if she could, bust out and leave everyone behind.

Egg knows this. She knows that Kathy is like dynamite —strike the match and your fingers burn, but you shouldn't play with matches. She knows that Kathy loves her but she hates her too. Not like hate-hate, not like Martin-hate. Kathy hates her like you hate the people who know you the best.

"Ostriches can live up to seventy years old," Egg calls out. Kathy does not move.

"They're so fast, they can go up to forty miles an hour."

Egg has told her this before but Kathy doesn't listen. Egg thinks that Kathy never listens. Egg shuffles up beside her sister and stuffs the cuff of her sleeve through the mesh. The ostrich pecks at the fabric. The ostrich blinks.

"See its eyes? They have a different kind of eyelid, they blink from side to side."

"Yeah," Kathy drawls, her nose wrinkling and Egg can smell the alfalfa. Kathy says, "And brains the size of walnuts." Kathy, who sweeps out the pens on weekends, tipping over the water trough and flushing out the slurry.

Egg knows that ostriches can be mean birds. They have that claw. To calm them, you put a sock over their heads. To calm them, you cover their eyes. Are the eyes too big for Kathy, and the neck, too flimsy, stretched out, too weak? Egg knows that Kathy hates the weak.

The ostrich booms, its pink neck inflated into a low *wooh-wooh-wooohhh*.

"Papa says they're runners, like the Road Runner on TV."

Kathy's fingers poke through the criss-cross geometry of the wire. Egg sees her taking in the pens, the fields, the shrinking slough by the side of the barn. She ponders the mysteries of her older, bigger sister. Kathy's gaze is far and away, her shoulders slump, as if the cast of the sky makes her smaller, as if the roll of the flatlands is crushing her.

"Kathy?"

Kathy looks at Egg and steps back. Her arm twitches and she reaches out to smooth down her sister's sprouting black tufts. "Come on," Kathy growls, as if to make up for the weak, "come on or we'll miss the bus."

Ostrich eggs are very strong. Egg has seen the dome they made in Montreal for the World's Fair Expo 67 from her *Young Reader's Guide to Science*. The Wave of the Future! Sit on an ostrich egg and it will not crack. The secret is they break from the inside.

. . .

The stone ridge stretches out at the beginning of the flats; the jutting rocks bleached white by a relentless sun. Riding at the back of the creaking school bus, Egg imagines the backbone of some long-dead creature. Here be dragons. This is dinosaur country after all. Egg loves the sweep of the prairie fields, that receding tide of grasslands, sculpted outcrops, the mysterious sentinels of the stone erratics. The sky, ever changing and eternal, is a boundless blue. Another ocean, Egg thinks. She likes the words *azure, aquamarine*.

She taps her heels together. She has a pencil case, bought with her own allowance, and a shiny new lunch tin, the one with Steve Austin, A Man Barely Alive. He was an astronaut in a horrible crash, but then they made him into the Six Million Dollar Man. Yes, Egg thinks, they can do that now, not like Humpty Dumpty at all.

Egg feels for the Six Million Dollar Man, but he is better than he was, faster and stronger. Sometimes when she runs, she can hear the music, the super-slow, super-strong, tick-tock of Bionic muscles. The Six Million Dollar Man has come through some hard times but he is happier than he was, just like a superhero. He has a secret life and he gets to save the world, over and over again.

He is like Evel Knievel that way. Evel Knievel is not a superhero but someone who was broken and made whole again. Evel Knievel has shattered every bone in his body and he can still ride his motorcycle. Egg knows that when they hit you, if it isn't broken, it doesn't matter. Sticks and stones. When the bullies come, that is what you are supposed to say. Sticks and stones may break my bones but names will never hurt me.

Egg whispers to herself. Names will never hurt me.

The bus rattles to a halt as the front doors wheeze open, filling the light with a swirl of dust. The ride is always better before the corner pickup, with the lazy rolling bump and jiggle of the gravel road. The corner pickup and Stacey Norman gets on board. Kathy leaps from her place beside Egg and slides into the seat beside Stacey near the front. Egg looks around for Albert but then she remembers that Albert will not be on the bus with her today. He will never be on the bus.

She clutches her new lunch box, feels the smooth plastic of the handle under her palm. At her feet sits her school bag, with her special notebook. She will write everything down, like in the empirical method. A notebook to figure things out, to make everything okay. First day and she will make sense of the world, just like the scientists do.

Mr. Johnston, the bus driver, fiddles with the dial and "Billy Don't Be a Hero" floats in from KQWP, radio Spokane, all the way from Washington. Egg rides into the small town of Bittercreek, past the dwindling houses and false-front shops on Main Street and the dilapidated grounds of the old stockyard. The churches and bars tumble by, Robertson's Repair-All and Gustafsson's General Store. Kathy says Bittercreek is so small you could spit from one end to the other and flat enough you could watch your dog run away for a week.

Egg taps her feet.

They are the only Japanese-Canadian family on the prairie, except for the mushroom farm way out in Nanton. Lethbridge is so far away, it doesn't even count, even if they do have the Japanese Garden. Coal River has the Lucky Dragon Café but they are Chinese and no one has an ostrich farm. The birds come all the way from Africa. Everyone is different but only white people are normal. Even the television says that.

They pull into the school parking lot, to the looming red brick and concrete, the biggest building in town, built for the Confederation centennial: Bittercreek Central School.

The doors of the bus fly open and the aisle is a mass of gangly legs, jutting elbows, the shove and holler as the stampede to the yard begins. Egg hunkers down and waits — the rush is like rattling stones in a soda pop can. When she hears, "Last one off is a dirty, rotten egg!" she stiffens, but no, that is not for her. With the big kids out of the way, Egg peeps her head above the green vinyl seats to make sure the coast is clear. Then she grabs her bookbag and lunch box.

Egg steps off the bus into the dazzle of light. First day of school and everything is new like a stack of birthday quarters. She taps her feet together. The blue whale has a heart the size of a car, and the speed of light is the fastest ever. These are facts. *Irrefutable.* Egg holds the word on her tongue as she steps towards the playground. The grit of the dirt crunches beneath her feet; she likes the shuffle-scratch sound. She takes a deep breath. The freshly mown scent of the football field tickles her nose and the white gravel of the baseball diamond actually seems to sparkle. A part of her, that twisty tight part of her deep in her chest, loosens ever so slightly as the warm brush of light glows against her skin. School is books too, the best Dictionary of all and Evangeline Granger in the library. A once upon a time and a happily ever after.

It's a new year and everything can be different.

There is a sting at her fingers, a jarring tug, and the handle of her lunch box is yanked away. The flash of her shiny tin

— Martin Fisken grins his fox grin, teeth bared, his laughter high and mocking. The sun glints on his flaxen hair. He smiles, his freckles seem to dance in delight across the bridge of his nose. Egg stands, stunned. There is no time, not even for surprise, as Martin kicks her brand new Six Million Dollar Man lunch box over the curb and into the gutter.

. . .

Egg thinks bumblebee bats. Bats the size of bumblebees. She knows they are the smallest mammal ever.

. . .

Egg straggles to the end of the line outside her classroom. She slouches, her shoulder slides against the wall, as if willing herself to blend into the painted cinder blocks. The screeches in the elementary school hallway careen off the concrete and granite. Cacophony, Egg thinks, like black crows against a barren field. She sticks her fingers into her ear sockets but she doesn't like the squeeze. She thinks of the world under water, of unbearable pressures, or copper-burnished diving helmets in the murky depths. If only she could be invisible! There are magic words — *abracadabra, presto magico* — she wills it — *shazam*!

"Come along." Egg feels Mrs. Syms's fingers claw into her shoulder, pushing her forward. "Idle hands do the Devil's work."

Mrs. Syms is Egg's grade two teacher. Mrs. Syms pinches.

Mrs. Malverna Syms, with frosty hair tied back in a bun, has taught elementary for as long as anyone can remember. Egg has heard her voice ringing out from the teacher's lounge: how she is soon to retire but how she loves the children. Mrs. Syms is a fairy tale grandmother, as if in a storybook, pictured with a gingerbread house behind her. As she walks the hallway with Vice Principal Geary by her side, Mrs. Syms talks of God's watchful care and how she is always vigilant for the sparrow's fall.

To Egg, Mrs. Syms towers, all jiggly jowls and flaring nostrils. Her fingers are curled like a raven's, and her eyes are a bloodless blue. Her hair, lashed back, is a bleak winter's grey.

The line trudges to the classroom before the bell, before the doors slam open and the older years rush through the corridor. In the hallways, Mrs. Syms uses her singsong voice but in the classroom it sounds very different.

"Children." Mrs. Syms's voice is flat as a ruler. "Silence." She slaps her pointer against the wall. Egg notes the strap hanging behind Mrs. Syms's desk — a dark brown leather cut from a worn crupper. She shudders.

Mrs. Syms continues, "I will now call out your last name and you will take your desk." She looks down at the attendance sheet. "Allen, Brennan, Brown." Her pointer, like some darting insect, hovers, then slashes to the front row.

Egg holds her breath.

"Collins, Cochran, Easton."

She grips the handle of her lunch box.

"Fisken."

The letters ring the room, above the chalkboard, beginning with A is for Apple. A is always for Apple. Egg knows this. It is never Apes or Apricots. Kathy says *Ah*pricots but Egg puts the apes in *Ape*pricots. Egg knows that if enough people say *Ape*pricots it will be real. Language is like that.

"Johnson, McClure, Murakami."

Her desk is right behind Martin. Martin Fisken: her nemesis. She slides into her chair ever so quietly, quelling her fear.

"Simpson, Taylor, Williams."

As Paulie Williams takes his seat behind Egg, she whips around and whispers, "Trade seats for two dollars?"

Paulie's eyebrows pop, like a jack-in-the-box weasel. He takes a moment to pull at his cowlick as he leans forward; he's a dead ringer for Dennis the Menace. "Two bucks every week," he says, as his eyes dart to the pursed lips of Mrs. Syms who peruses her attendance sheet.

Egg squints. "One buck one week, a Tootsie Roll the next." She knows that he favours the sticky caramels and taffies that he can pull into strings. He has lost two fillings already, rattling them in his daddy's tobacco tin that he keeps in his back pocket.

"Sponge toffee," he counters.

She gives a curt nod, "Deal," and slips sideways out of her seat. Luck is with her, for at that moment Mrs. Syms turns to the blackboard, writing her name with great sweeping letters against the pristine slate. Egg nods to Paulie — she is halfway to his seat, her arms already on his desk. Beside them, little Jimmy Simpson raises his eyebrows but he does not say a word. It's a smooth swap all around.

At least now she is closer to the back of the class and she has something between her and Martin Fisken. A dollar is worth it. That and sponge toffee. She holds her breath when Mrs. Syms looks over her classroom but no, her teacher does not suspect a thing.

Egg rocks back in relief.

Last December Martin Fisken chased Egg down the hall, shouting that she killed Pearl Harbour. Egg always gets chased at Pearl Harbour — that was when the Japs were evil. But for now, December is an eternity away, just as August is long past. For

Egg, December and August are the hardest months. In August, Martin and his gang caught her by Gustafsson's store with the worst game of all, something he called Atomic Bomb—the knees and elbows hurt the most. Grown-ups tell you to turn the other cheek, but that doesn't help if the blows keep coming. In the Greek myths, Nemesis is the Goddess of Retributive Justice but Egg knows that nemesis in the Dictionary means something different. Egg had to look up the word retributive. Sometimes the Dictionary is like a puzzle, going from word to word, like the thread in the Minotaur's labyrinth. If you don't know one word, you have to look up another, until the meaning is all unravelled.

For Egg, it is all very complicated. The Greeks were scientists but without the science. They knew about atoms but they couldn't see them. That's what Democritus said; Egg read it in her *Young Reader's Guide to Science.* So the atoms were like stories you made up and now we know that atoms are real.

The Greeks didn't have Jesus. Science or no science, Mrs. MacDonnell in Sunday School says the Greeks are going to Hell.

Egg looks up. The pointer is out. Everyone knows about Mrs. Syms and the pointer. But Mrs. Syms stands by her desk and places her hand on a stack of books. Her fingers drum, a cascade of clicks as her nails skitter off the cover.

"Now children," Mrs. Syms holds up a book, "this year we will be reading *Charlotte's Web*." Every front row desk gets a pile. "Take one and pass them back."

Her heart jumps when Martin slaps the books on Paulie's desk but he quickly turns back; he has taken no notice of the switch. Even Paulie just slides the book behind him without a second glance.

Relieved, Egg picks up the slender volume, strokes the cover: a girl, staring dreamily into the distance, a spider's web, a pig.

Egg knows the story for Kathy has read it to her already. Kathy goes for the stories where children fly and wise animals talk, magical and miraculous, but Egg reads the Dictionary, her favourite book. She likes the brevity and precision. The Dictionary makes sense of the world, the A to Z of it, defined and ordered. Everything else is so muddled. Egg stares at the flap of skin beneath Mrs. Syms's chin and she thinks of the turkey's waddle and gobble. She sits straight up in her chair, palms on the desk, alert and ready. Not that she is browner, no. As Mrs. Syms speaks to the class, enunciating her *d*'s, *t*'s, and *i-n-g*'s, Egg looks over her fellow students: Martin Fisken, Chuckie Buford, Glenda, and all the same gang from last year. She spreads her fingers, feels the desk, solid, the chair. She knows that wood has grains but not like sand. Egg sits. She thinks of the word *diaphanous. Mutual of Omaha's Wild Kingdom* says that animals can smell fear, like blood in the water; they can sense it from miles away.

Paulie raises his hand and he is off to the washroom.

Egg gazes at Martin's head, his slender neck and wispy blond hair. The fuzz on the back of his head is like the softest down on the head of an ostrich chick. She starts at that unexpected fragility, at the curve of the skull that seems so much like a shell. She thinks of the ear's spiral, how ears and noses are the strangest things and even if you leave them out of your drawings, your faces won't turn out creepy. Martin's little dog ears make him look smaller. A curl of his lips brings out a snarl. Egg wonders what makes the mean come out in people, if it is there all the time, like the appendix, or is it something you catch, like the cooties? Can we cut it out, the badness in ourselves, if we turn the other cheek?

Martin Fisken twists around in his chair. His freckles, sprinkled across the bridge of his nose, remind her of sparkles on the Christmas cupcakes, the faded red on shortbread cookies. With his smile and golden hair, he could be on a Weetabix box. The thought vanishes when he leans towards Egg and whispers, "This year, Jap, this year, you are going to die."

. . .

At the first clang of the lunch bell, Egg bolts out of the classroom. Run run run as fast as you can, you can't catch me, I'm the gingerbread man. That's how the story goes. She skulks behind the monkey bars, close to the bushes. By the bushes, at least, she can blend in with the runts, she is small enough. She knows the art of camouflage; she's seen it on the *Mutual of Omaha's Wild Kingdom*, the fawns in the tall grasses, the nestlings in the trees. Stillness is the key.

In the schoolyard she can hear the chant:

> *my mother and your mother*
> *were hanging up the clothes*
> *my mother punched your mother*
> *right in the nose*
> *what colour was the blood?*
> *r - e - d spells red*
> *so out you must go*
> *with your mother's*
> *big fat toe*
> *not because you're dirty*

not because you're clean
just because you kissed a boy
behind the ma-ga-zine

She scans the yard. At first all seems chaotic, the rush and swirl of bodies at rest and in motion, but she can pick out the patterns. Hopscotch is for girls, along with skipping and the *clap clap clap* of Miss Mary Mack. With the boys it's all tag and spud and the monkey in the middle. Each grade has its own territory, within their elementary, middle, and high school sections. In the high school grounds, the divisions are clearer—how the hand-me-down shirts vie with the store-bought denim, how the princess girls flirt with the Popular jocks. The brainers hover by the glass doors of the library, far away from the shouts and squeals of the playground. In the playground the runts climb over the tangle of the jungle gym, where it is the survival of the fittest.

I'm the king of the castle
you're the dirty rascal

Here, behind the bushes, Egg is safe and sound. She squats and places her lunch box in front of her. Her hand strokes the scratches on the Six Million Dollar Man's face. She will not cry. Steve Austin never cried. She will stop being stupid. She will stop being weak.

She opens her lunch box to the neat rice balls, folded within the black *nori* squares. Her mother's *onigiri*. Only you can't have onigiri in the lunchroom. Or anything smelly, or sticky, or easy-peasy japa-nesy. That is the kiss of death.

Mutual of Omaha says that the predators cull the herd, that they only take the weak. This is the law of the jungle. Across the yard, Kathy stands with all her friends. Debbie Duncan squeals and rushes forward; she is all bubbling excitement, bobbed blond curls and Bonne Bell lips. Raymond is there, with a shirt that is too city; he is thin and fine in a way that gets him into trouble. Egg's word for Raymond is *debonair*—a dash of French to make it all interesting. Jillian Henderson, the constable's daughter, saunters up with a "Hey, Kathy! Last year, senior. We'll rule the roost."

Kathy is not a princess girl, but she is still Popular, even after things went bad with Albert and everything. Kathy is still the captain of the basketball team, even if it is just for girls, Kathy standing on the green when everyone knows that the grass is for the jocks, Kathy, who smokes in the coulee, down by the splinter-dry cottonwoods and sage, Kathy, who breaks all the rules anyway.

There is a shout from the rough-and-tumble shinny in the yard. Doug Fisken, his stick in the air, runs by a cheering Per Stinton. Townies. The big bullies. Kathy and her friends draw closer.

Kathy isn't careful. Even Superman has his kryptonite. Egg has the comics to prove it. And Albert, the star of the baseball team, a no-hitter pitcher at the regional championships and that was two seasons running. Egg blinks against the glare and squats behind the stunted bushes.

They say accidents are nobody's fault. Albert's accident. His fall from the railway trestle over the fast-flowing river.

Was he trying to fly?

liar liar pants on fire
hang your clothes on a telephone wire

Egg gazes down the street to the intersection of Maple and Main Streets. She can barely make out the corner of the old stockyard. She runs across the playground, to the field, dashing under the bleachers beside the track. Up she goes, her feet a *tap tap tap* on the stairs. From the top bench she can see the spread of the entire town.

Queen Street, Logan, Victoria Drive. The churches, the hardware store, the scratch of dirt roads against prairie fields. Egg scans the indifferent horizon; the sky has no face.

Albert, Albert, where are you?

She turns back to the school.

In the yard, the princess girls flutter from circle to circle. They have bright coloured blouses with frills and lace and sometimes dresses of organdy and chiffon. Egg wears her dungarees. She loves her dungarees. Kathy wears her blue jeans and her summer shirt with snap buttons. Egg wants snap buttons when she gets older. She looks across the grey crackled concrete and feels the itch in the palm of her hands. It is the first day and she needs some answers. First day and you don't want to be the goat. First day, and whatever happens now, happens forever.

Egg bites her lip.

Kathy doesn't fit in. But she gets along all right, even without the dresses. How does she do that?

Egg rubs the worn patches on her knees, and stares at her white shirt and running shoes with the blue laces. She doesn't look too different. But she knows. She walks down the bleachers, her steps heavy, and shuffles to the garbage. She throws her onigiri into the bin. She has to make some sacrifices. She stares down at the white rice balls, the black nori even as her stomach twists with hunger. Sacrifices. Like Steve Austin.

The Japanese part has got to go.

. . .

There is peace in the library. Egg likes the quiet. She likes the books arranged in alphabetical order, the corridor of shelves, the soft tread of the carpet. There are secret places that no one goes, the corner of Philosophy and Ancient History, the aisle from Afghanistan to Upper Volta. Upper Volta has a capital called Ouagadougou. Egg likes all the vowels. In the library, the shelves are cluttered, the aisles narrow, but to Egg this is a comfort. The light is dim, a dance of dust motes, the windows high on the wall above the dark panelled wood. The library is small but as she steps inside, the space blooms out and deepens. For Egg, the library is like magic. It is like going into the swimming pool from the shallow end, stepping deeper and deeper until the water is over her head but without all the scariness and without all the wet. Egg does not like the wet. In summertime, she had her swimming lessons and the sound bounced off the walls. Martin Fisken pushed her into the pool and she coughed when she swallowed the water. Sometimes the water burned her eyes but then she could say she was not really crying. Here, Egg can tuck herself behind the book cart and slip into the lowest shelf, she is so small, but there is no need, not today. At the beginning of the year, the library is empty. There is only Miss Granger, stamping and re-stamping the cards, filing the books away.

Egg has read the Andersen, the Aesop, and the Grimm, and knows the forest, deep and dark, the path of wolves and thorns, but it is the myths she likes the best: the boy who flew too close to the sun, the monster in the labyrinth. Enchantments, the trials and tests and fabulous beasts! And the names! Athena, Artemis, and Aphrodite! Galatea and Persephone! A goddess of wisdom and a goddess of beauty and each Muse with her own wonderful gift. The Gods, who were not so wise, nor just, not even particularly good but merely powerful and at the same time pitifully weak. And Pandora's box — Egg wonders — what does it mean when hope is the one thing left inside?

The library has all the answers.

And yet, as Egg searches through the shelves, she can find no books on her Japanese. A history of Japan and the Second World War, but no Japanese, here, in Canada. No Japanese like herself.

"Egg?"

She turns to Miss Granger who stands in the aisle. Miss Granger, who has the most beautiful name: Evangeline. Her dark hair is swept back and her dress is a washed-out brown. She is young, barely twenty, or something like twenty; Egg can't gauge the age of grown-ups. Yet there is something about Evangeline that suggests a sepia-toned past, as if she has stepped out of an old-time photograph. Egg remembers that last year, Evangeline was all in asters, a blossom of violets and forget-me-nots — when Albert was still alive. In this moment, Egg wishes she had brought something for Evangeline. There is a sweetness to her that gives Egg the shivers and Egg so much wants to make her smile.

"How is your first day going?" Evangeline asks.

Egg bites her lip. "Mrs. Syms is my teacher now."

Evangeline sighs. It is then Egg knows that Mrs. Syms has not fooled everyone.

"First day is always the longest." Evangeline places her hand on Egg's shoulder, the lightest touch. Egg can see the crescent moons on fingernails bitten to the quick. "But it's not forever," Evangeline adds.

Grown-ups always say this. It doesn't help. Like "you'll understand when you get older." Like a cookie jar placed just out of her reach.

But Evangeline, her jagged nails, her soothing voice, she has always been kind. She smiles with a warmth that spreads to her eyes, and asks, "What colour would you like today?" They walk behind the counter where Evangeline keeps her rainbow of lollipops, stashed behind the stamps and her stack of blank book slips. Last year, on the bad days, Evangeline would slip a candy to her. Egg does not think it strange that the school librarian would know her bad days. She has read of guardian angels and Evangeline is everything angelic.

Evangeline, Evangeline, Egg wants to sing her name.

Click click click. She twirls the candy against the back of her teeth. Evangeline is showing her two new books: *From the Mixed-Up Files of Mrs. Basil E. Frankweiler*—a strange title, Egg thinks—and *A Wrinkle in Time.*

Click. Her tongue will be purple.

"How is your family?" Evangeline asks.

Egg's throat tightens. She thinks of Papa, exiled to the ostrich barn, and how could she explain Mama? Her tears almost rise, her chest so full. It is too much to be on the outside, the only Japanese family on the prairie with Albert dead and Kathy with the snap buttons and herself with the lunch box onigiri. Everything is upside down and jumbled. Yet Evangeline, her brown eyes and lollipops, Egg wants to tell her—no, she wants to run away, to hide behind the wooden cart. Here, in the library, Egg wants the books to swallow her.

"Perfect," she says.

As Evangeline turns to her stacks, Egg realizes that no one must know, of Mama's whiskey, of Papa's cot, of Martin chasing her, taunting *jap jap jap*. Egg thinks of Pandora, of all the evils in the world contained in one box. A secret. She will not be like Pandora. She will bury it.

Evangeline Granger looks so much like a storybook heroine, like Laura Ingalls in *Little House on the Prairie*. Her family has been in Bittercreek since before the railroad. There is even a road, off Four Corners, named after the first Granger in the territory. Evangeline, daughter of Old Man Granger, the sourest man east of the Rockies. She is like a pioneer girl in a bonnet. Egg, on her tiptoes, so much wants to ask her how it is to be normal, how it is to be white.

. . .

At the end of the day, the bell rings through the corridors. The bus will be leaving soon. At her desk, Egg sits, as her fellow students rush out of the classroom. She bites her lip. She will not be the goat, not this year. She will wait and run just before the bus pulls out of the parking lot. Then Martin Fisken will not be able to catch her. She's been practising all summer long.

She looks down at her legs and taps her feet together. If she were taller, she'd be able to run like the ostriches. She tries to imagine her legs growing, pulled long like taffy. Egg knows you must be careful what you wish for—that's in the stories as well. As the last of the class bolts out the door, she grabs her bag and rises.

At the door, she looks up and down the hall. Now she will take the long way, into the high school corridor, that is her plan. She dashes down the hallways, by the rows and rows of lockers, through labyrinthine twists and turns. Her footsteps echo, bouncing against the glass and granite and the dull concrete.

She stops. She looks down the empty passageway, the light a watery fluorescence.

She is lost.

"Hey squirt."

Egg jerks her head up but it is only Raymond, who smiles when he calls her that.

"What are you doing up here?" he asks. "Are you looking for your sister?"

Egg nods. Raymond, in his city shirt, should be on *Soul Train*, not trapped in this dust bowl of Bittercreek. He gazes at her and for a moment Egg wonders if Kathy has spoken to him about her — the weak one. The small one. The stupid one who can barely talk in class.

Raymond leans forward. "When I had Mrs. Syms, she scared the bejesus out of me. She still does. I couldn't even go to the bathroom. I swear, all year I looked like a penguin," and he walks for her, his knees locked together. They laugh and Egg wonders. A part of her is amazed that he would give that away, a story that makes him look so weak. Is there a word for that? Egg gazes at his dark eyes and fine features, as he waves goodbye and makes his way down the hall. He is the only boy that she would call beautiful. She knows that Doug Fisken calls him sissyface, the football team snickers when he walks down the hall. Egg wants to catch up to him and ask him why.

"Egg," Kathy is suddenly beside her. "How was the day?"

Egg nods. If you don't say anything, it's not like you are really lying. "Miss Granger gave me the *Mixed-Up Files* and some *Wrinkle in Time*."

"I loved those books." But Kathy spies Egg's dented lunch box, the long scratch where the paint is scored off. "What happened?" she asks.

Egg's voice drops. "I fell, an accident." She clears her throat and gallops off with, "We're learning about the Vast Open Plains of the Northern Tundra!"

"Oh Egg," Kathy chides, so much like a big sister, "you've got to be more careful."

Egg sinks into her chest and all the words come tumbling inside her: *stupid clumsy useless dumbbell.* She must be as vigilant as the nestlings on the Savannah. Yes. She must be more careful.

. . .

Egg steps off the school bus and drags her bookbag behind her. She shuffles her feet and kicks at the gravel in the drive. She thinks of her Greek myths, of a man carrying the world on his shoulders, or the one rolling the rock uphill. She looks at the barn, the house, the field. The sun beats down on the parched grass by the shrinking slough. She feels the heat loosening, as if unravelling—this is *her* barn, *her* house, *her* field—and sighs a small relief that the first day of school is over. Her shoulders sag, as if all the bad of the day drains out of her.

Bye bye Martin Fisken. So long Snooty Syms.

Egg turns to the barn, holds her head up to the scent of green: alfalfa hay. It smells like Mama's fragrant tea leaves in the black lacquered bowl. She can see her Mama through the kitchen window, the frame squeezing her smaller and smaller.

The sonorous boom of the ostrich call fills the late afternoon air. Two ostriches, a black plume and a smaller brown plume weave from side to side in their outdoor pen. Their kantling dance, the awkward loping, wings stretched wide, that ridiculous bobbing head as the neck flails from side to side — Egg knows that this is ostrich S - E - X. From what Egg knows of S - E - X, she thinks it is just stupid.

She makes her way into the barn. As she opens the gate, her eyes scan the three indoor pens that line the south side. There are two pens for the adult ostriches (one for each breeding pair) and each pen has a grill that opens to the outside enclosure. The last pen is for the chicks' run. Egg drops her bag, hears the *glug glug* of the jerry can, and turns. Her father fills the water trough, twisting the spout in the corner. He looks up and gives her a nod. Papa's movements are precise, just enough and nothing extra. His features are sharp, as if cut by a razor, his frame is wiry, with a strength that compacts and contains. In her father, there are pressures of time and the patience of ages. Like the glaciers, Egg thinks, like the erratics. As she climbs onto the stool by the old wood stove, she catches the swing of her legs by hooking her ankles on the bar. She knows he likes the calm, how he wraps himself up in a cocoon of quiet. Butterflies come from cocoons. Egg knows that bears hibernate, that frogs come from tadpoles after a string of jelly eggs. *Metamorphosis.* The word sits on the tip of her tongue.

His cot, neatly made, is tucked in by the boxes at the back of the barn. Albert's boxes. Albert's room is empty now. Like a hole where the heart used to be.

"How was your first day of school?" Papa asks.

"Good," Egg chirps. He would expect nothing less.

Her father lays out the pellets and alfalfa in a pan to lure the first pen into the barn. He gives a piercing whistle to announce that the feed is in. The ostriches, with their awkward stick-like gait, make their way towards the pan, their necks scooping and curving. When they are all inside, her father latches the grill behind them.

Egg straightens. "Can I get the eggs? I'll be extra careful."

"All right."

Egg slips off her stool and runs outside to the pens. The wind rises, lifting as it gathers force, funnelling down the foothills to roar across the plains. Tumbleweed clouds in a churning sky. Through the wire gate, she dashes to the scratched-out nest and scoops out the two large eggs, one in each arm. She braces them against her chest, cradles the bulk of them, these strange, stone-like spheres. "Metamorphosis," she whispers. She walks back inside the barn, her footsteps slow and cautious as the wind makes mischief of her hair. She places these treasures into her father's arms. As he wipes the eggs clean, he strokes the rough, pitted pores of the shell. He holds, feels the weight in his palm.

"Look," he murmurs. Arm extended, he candles the egg, clicks on his flashlight, and casts the beam upward. Lit from below, he traces the thin outline of the air sac, the yellow glow of the yolk. A satisfied grunt sounds from his throat. He places the egg on the setting tray, the slight point of the shell down, with the concave curve of the air cell at the top. He pencils in the date, a bumpy scrawl.

Egg rocks back on her heels, then taps them together. When her father laughs, it is like air leaking out of him, but that was before Albert's accident. He was bigger then, a thousand feet taller. To Egg, it seems as if he is shrinking, shrinking to fit the smallness under the beams, drawing in the shadows of the barn and the pens.

Egg would like to ask him why he won't leave the ostrich barn but she can't quite get out the words. It's like her mouth is full of gumballs, so sour she can't even spit. There are a million questions she would like to ask: Why does their family have to be so different? Why does different feel so wrong?

Was it always this way? No, not until Albert died.

The kettle whistles on the stove. Sharp.

He takes his mason jars from the box by the door and fills them with the hot water, capping the lids with a firm twist. The jars he places around the setting tray. Patiently, he wraps a rolled blanket around the edges of the tray to keep in the warmth for as long as possible: his makeshift incubator for the next forty days.

He is an ostrich Papa, Egg thinks. Albert was the boy, he was everything. The rest of us don't matter.

"The chicks are filling up the crate, Dad," Egg points to the male and female ostriches, their necks poking through the bars. "Gertie and Bertie, their feathers look thicker. And Griszelda—"

"Shouldn't give them names, Egg. You know that." There is a lilt to his voice, the slightest accent.

Egg bites her lip and repeats his old admonishment, "Can't get too attached."

Papa nods.

Behind him, at the back of the barn, behind the low tangle of thin wire, the ostrich chicks call from their brooder crate, a high trilling whinny. At a few weeks, their down is not quite feather, still blunted; the full majestic mass of plumage is yet to come. Egg clicks her tongue and watches as their heads perk, rising on their elongated necks like comical telescopes.

Ostrich Papa squats in front of the pen, peering at the chicks. Ostrich Papa, so close he can see only the hatchlings. Candling and turning his clutch.

Egg swallows past the tightness in her throat. "Can I run them?" she asks.

"You have to sweep the pen first," Papa says. Egg goes to the corner that holds the rakes, pitchfork, and the spiky rust-harrow that gives her nightmares. She draws out the wide broom that has been cut to her size.

As she sweeps out the chicks' pen, her father checks his breeders: the four small females, their brown coats dull in the afternoon light. The two black-feather ostrich males, with their ridge of white feathers, have lost some weight in this season. Their pink necks bulge as they commence their evening call. *Wooh-wooh-wooohhh.* Egg lays down the hessian jute and spreads the grit for their gizzards. Jute, for the traction, and the grit, to help grind the feed in their stomachs. With the hatchlings, they will have to be careful. Infection, impaction, dehydration, and diarrhea, although the loop of twine between the legs may take care of the spraddle. The losses are high with the young ones. She eyes the floor for a stray piece of straw, an errant threat that could catch in their throats—because the ostriches will eat anything. Papa has wrapped the lower sides of the chick pen with fine wire for the bars are too wide to hold them in. Egg lays out the shallow pan of feed. As she opens the side of the crate, the chicks tumble out, at times their long legs splaying underneath the weight of their bodies. The biggest ones are nearly half her size. She stands, and stares, and feels the uncomplicated pull of their companionship, their animal nature. They are innocent, after all. Their chirps are a simple *me! me! me!* that pulls at her heart. Palms out, she feels them pass beneath her hands, the tickle of fuzz and incipient feathers as they scamper to the pan.

. . .

After dinner, Mama takes one look at Egg, at the yellow husks in her hair and the smear of Godknowswhat on her forehead, and declares that it is bath time.

As she sheds her clothes, Egg thinks *metamorphosis.*

In the bathtub, she ducks her head under the water and all the sounds of the house come booming, so close and so far. It is like she is inside herself. She holds her breath. A water cocoon. She knows that the blue whale is the biggest animal ever, in all of existence, even bigger than any dinosaur. At two hundred tons, its heart is as big as a car and it breathes through a blowhole. The blue whale, who can live a hundred years, older than elephants, they roam the oceans but no one knows where. What must they think of the sky, that other ocean, the harsh and alien air, something you need to live but you can't quite live in?

Egg wonders what they dream.

Ostriches dream. They tuck their heads beneath their wings but they don't fly. Sometimes they shudder and when the wind comes up, they dance in circles, feathers spread and spindly legs kicking. Their heads bob and weave. Egg, in the bath with her head underwater, thinks about ostriches. She wonders. No one else has an ostrich farm.

Kathy scoops her up from the tub, tousling Egg's wet hair with her blue towel, her Ninny Blankie with the corners chewed, but that was when Egg was a baby. After teeth brushing and pjs, Kathy tucks Egg into bed. With a snap of the wrist, Kathy floats the sheet down the length of the bed and draws the edge under Egg's chin.

Egg laughs. "You're like a magician."

Kathy scoops the *moufu,* the heavy blanket, from the foot of the bed and plops it down on Egg's head. It is like an old game of avalanche.

Egg's head pops from beneath the blanket. "You going out with Stacey tonight?"

"Yeah. What about it?" Kathy, straightening out the corners of the bed, has her prickles up.

Egg sighs. She knows that her sister will keep her secrets until the day she dies but they are written all over her face. "Nothing...Could you tell me a story?"

"Egg—"

"A short one. Promise not to interrupt." Egg crosses her heart. "Hope to die."

Kathy puffs out her cheeks.

"Or I can tell you about the Vast Open Plains of the Northern—"

"Okay, okay," Kathy rubs her chin, "give me a sec."

Egg sits and draws the blanket around her. "Is Papa ever coming out of the ostrich barn?"

"I don't know."

"Kathy?"

"Yeah?" Kathy's hand pats the bottom of the bed for Neko-neko, Egg's puppet Kitty. Egg can't sleep without Nekoneko.

"How did you get Popular?"

"Well, I don't know that I'm Popular."

"No one teases you, and I've seen you stand up for Raymond."

"Is that what this is about? Is someone teasing you? Is it Martin?"

Egg sinks a little. "No." She worries the corner of the moufu. "I just wish things were different."

Kathy pulls out Nekoneko from beneath the bed and knocks off the dust. "Yeah," she says softly.

Humpty Dumpty, Egg thinks.

"It's time for you to go to sleep." Kathy raises her hand to the lamp but her eyes fall to the book on the bedside table. "Hey," she says as she picks up the worn paperback of *Anne Frank: Diary of a Young Girl*. "If you want me to read this to you, don't read ahead, okay?" She squints at Egg. "Have you been going through my room again?"

Egg hugs the book to her chest. "I just like to hold it. Let me keep it, please—I won't read ahead, I promise. I just like to look at her picture." Egg rubs the outline of Anne's photograph at the back of the book and thinks of her own notebook. It's the first day of school and her pages are blank but she is too tired and enough is enough. Egg rolls onto her back and sighs. "I would like a best friend, Kathy."

Kathy turns off the lamp.

Egg tosses dramatically. "I can't sleep."

Kathy strokes Egg's head, her fingers threading through her thick, stubborn hair. She whispers, "Just think of all the alphabet animals."

Egg closes her eyes. The first day of school. The first September without Albert. She thinks of Mama and retreats into her blanket. "Do you think we're broken?"

"Shh, Egg. Shh."

Egg feels the lulling motion of Kathy's hand stroking her hair, hears the rhythm of Kathy's breathing. Through her window, she can see the swirl of constellations. She thinks of the big blue whale, a pod of leaping dolphins—and Raymond—she smiles. If penguin Raymond can make it through school, maybe Egghead ostriches can too.

She sleeps.

. . .

Egg opens her eyes. The moonlight falls through her window. The curtains waver, stirred by the faintest draft in this quiet, quiet dark.

Quiet. But no. That sound.

Egg sits up.

She hears a cry from down the hall. Mama's room. Egg darts to her door, the shock of the cold floor on her bare feet making her run faster and faster, a tiptoe mouse scurry to the bedroom down the hall. She pauses at her Mama's door and peeks through the crack.

Mama slumps by the side of the bed, her back to Egg. Her hands are clasped in prayer.

"Why, Albert?" Mama sobs.

Egg steps back, steps away. She thinks of her father in the ostrich barn, of Kathy—Egg jerks towards the shadows of her sister's open bedroom door—Kathy is still out with Stacey. Mama cries, Mama cries but Egg cannot go to her. Egg is frozen, like the Vast Open Plains of the Northern Tundra. First day of school and Albert was not with them. Albert will never be with them. He has been dead for three months, two weeks, and five days — such a long, long time. Now they are all broken apart and Mama's lost and drifting and all the king's horses and all the king's men will never be able to put them back together again.

Egg runs back to her room, to her bed. She pulls the covers over her head. She does not want to see, she does not want to hear. She feels her heart shrivel up in her chest, a small, hard thing, not like the blue whale at all. The blue whale will not help her; not even the speed of light will bring Albert back. She curls and tucks her knees up to her chin and thinks of the stolen mints from the drawer, the matches from her Papa's tool box. She cannot be good. And if she is not good, then she is damned.

Egg knows that Mama wants Albert. But Egg is alive and Albert isn't.

October

Time crawls in the classroom. It is not even lunchtime and it already feels like forever. As Egg looks out the window, she can see the low-lying clouds streaking against a duller grey. The trees have begun shedding their leaves, the fields fading slowly to yellow. Egg wiggles in her chair. She's placed *The Mixed-Up Files* and *A Wrinkle in Time* on the corner of her desk for her lunchtime library trek.

Egg likes Claudia and Jamie in the *From the Mixed-Up Files of Mrs. Basil E. Frankweiler*, their idea to live in the Metropolitan Museum of Art in New York City, although Egg would have chosen the big Eaton's in Calgary instead. It's a good story — research — if ever she should run away. Money and a good bed: these are important. Egg thinks that the most important thing about running away is not the away part. The most important thing is the destination, the running to, or it all just becomes about running and that's another kind of stuck. Also, violin cases are handy to pack your clothes.

Stories are imagination. Stories aren't real. But stories tell us something, don't they, even if they are fiction? That's what troubles Egg. That Claudia Kincaid is so real.

In math, she raises her hand to go to the bathroom.

Egg takes the long way around. You're not supposed to take the long way around, but sometimes, especially during junior recess, Egg takes the hallway into the high school wing. Kathy has a new English teacher called Miss Chapman who has a whole bunch of new words that Egg is trying to wrap her head around. She likes onomatopoeia but oxymoron makes her laugh. Kathy says that Egg collects words like dogs collect bones. As Egg peers into Miss Chapman's classroom, she sees this new teacher at the front of her class.

The older you get, you either fatten or you shrivel, that's what Kathy says. Egg watches Miss Chapman at the blackboard; her writing slants and slashes—the *y*'s drop like daggers and the *v*'s leap off the slate. *Dostoyevsky Tolstoy Chekhov.* Miss Chapman stands rigid, in a charcoal dress, her midnight-black hair in a blunt bowl cut. Her fingernails are ruby red, stark against the chalk. Snow White's stepmother. Egg can see that Miss Chapman is not shrunken nor shrivelled but compressed and contained. The forces of gravity are working on Miss Chapman. She could go off at any second.

Grown-ups are a mystery. Principal Crawley has a thin mustache, beady eyes, and a weasel's twitch. Vice Principal Geary is always clutching his pockets, his fingers thick as sausages. Everyone knows that Vice Principal Geary will come in drunk at least once during the semester and blubber during the Easter play. It is best to stay away from his bratwurst fingers. Mrs. Ayslin, skittish in her long summer sleeves, is always hovering on the edge of the teacher's assembly. Mrs. Ayslin will sport a shiner after Christmas break, always running into a wall, a door, whatever is handy, everyone knows.

It's grown-ups who play pretend most of all.

Miss Chapman's voice pierces the air. "Now why does Ivan Ilyich feel such torment? He's dying, but why at that moment?"

All heads are bowed.

"Debbie."

Debbie Duncan, Kathy's friend. Debbie's mum takes in the wash for the Crawleys and Stintons and Fiskens. Her father is nowhere to be found.

Debbie falters, "Sorry, Mrs. Chapman. I wasn't—"

"That's *Ms*. Ms. Chapman," she cuts in, "and no, you weren't."

Egg stares at the curve of Ms. Chapman's eyebrows, the twist of her lips. Ms. Chapman, from outside Bittercreek. They do things differently there.

Ms. Chapman's head swivels and snaps. "Kathy. What about Ivan Ilyich? His torment?"

Kathy unfurls herself from her don't-pick-me slouch. "Ah, it's the world that he's in, it's so hypocritical, and it's—he had his chance but he blew it." Chapman turns, a dismissal but Kathy continues, "It doesn't seem fair though, like he only had this one chance then—"

"Fair has nothing to do with it." Chapman clicks and rattles. "Irrevocable moments. But he chooses, he chooses not to save himself. Character is destiny," she proclaims. She whips out her last statement and slams it down like a cosmic gavel.

Character is destiny. Egg furrows her brow. How is that so? Character is character and destiny is destiny. That's why they have different words. Kathy has told her that metaphors are lies that tell the truth but what's the truth in that?

At the end of the day, Egg slaps the blackboard brushes together by the pencil sharpener. She doesn't mind the chores. This keeps her out of harm's way until the school bus pickup and maybe Mrs. Syms won't be so mean. Fresh pencil smell but the chalk dust makes her sneeze. Egg likes to sneeze. The heart stops when you sneeze, that's why you say "Bless you." She empties the cylindrical sharpener and pokes her fingers through the different sized holes. The sharpener is like the sausage maker down at Gustafsson's, only in reverse. Reverse and opposite are kind of like the same but not.

Egg dashes to the open doors of the school bus. Mr. Johnston, the bus driver, must be in the teacher's lounge scrounging up a cup of coffee and maybe even one of Mrs. McCracken's home-made butter biscuits. Egg scans the schoolyard. Martin Fisken is nowhere in sight. But she can see Kathy on the basketball court, showing off for Stacey. All the rest of the bus kids are far to the other side of the yard, by the picnic tables or on the jungle gym; their squeals bounce off the concrete. Egg looks back at her sister, at Stacey, who waits on the sidelines. The late autumn light blazes behind them, two silhouettes made smaller by the crush of the sky. Kathy holds the ball in her hands, standing in the free throw circle. Egg watches, waits for her sister to take that shot. But the shot never comes. Why, Egg wonders, why is Kathy just standing there? Egg feels a sudden sense of things beyond her grasp. She wants to call out to her sister, to shout some warning, for Kathy seems so lost and alone. But Kathy is not alone. Stacey slowly walks onto the court. It seems to Egg that it takes Stacey a long time to reach her sister. Kathy, head down, stares at the ground, her body small, as if she has folded something precious, tucked it up inside herself and hidden it away. She stands so still. But Stacey just walks out to Kathy and places her hands on Kathy's face, brings her chin up. Egg sees the ball fall away, bump bump bump bump bump. It rolls unevenly across the court.

The afternoon light, the shift and flare. Egg can't tell exactly what she has seen.

Mr. Johnston's whistle blasts as he strides towards the bus, the spring in his step sloshing the coffee over the rim of his mug. He stuffs a shortbread cookie in his mouth, as he jangles the keys. The kids come streaming from the yard, pouring off the jungle gym. They run towards the bus, all shouts and screams. The floor jounces beneath Egg's feet. She looks back to the basketball court. But the moment has passed and Kathy and Stacey have already joined the raucous line to the bus doors.

Mr. Johnston pulls the lever and then they are off.

At the house Egg rushes to her room and slides under the bed with a pencil and paper, pushing the bits of Lego and rolling the dinky cars away. *Character is destiny.* That means if you change who you are, you change what happens. *Metamorphosis.* Egg thinks of Claudia Kincaid in *From the Mixed-Up Files of Mrs. Basil E. Frankweiler.* Claudia needed a mystery to uncover, to complete her adventure. Claudia needed a mystery to solve, to come back changed.

This makes Egg wonder.

Kathy says fairy tales are stories told to children so they can learn about the world. The Moral of the Story is Don't be So Stupid like in Little Red Riding Hood or Don't be So Greedy like in Goldilocks and the Three Bears. Egg's favourite story is Rumpelstiltskin. You would think the hero would be the queen but she didn't do anything, just cried until Rumpel came around and saved her butt. He was the one who could spin straw into gold. The king was the evil one, telling her that if she didn't spin the straw into gold he would kill her, and he got all the gold in the end. Kathy says that is called Capitalism.

Egg is not quite sure what the Moral of the Story is.

In an adventure tale, you can be a Hero or a Damsel Fair. But not both. Girls are never heroes. In an adventure story, someone is saved. The dragon is slain. The moral is that good triumphs over evil, just like in real life.

The Greeks didn't have morals. Or maybe it's just Get Out of the Way of the Gods. Egg thinks that the story of Job in the Bible is like that. He is rewarded in the end with a new wife and new kids but what about the old wife and old kids? They didn't do anything wrong and they were smoted, just like that. What if Job liked his old wife better? And Egg wonders what the old wife thought about how things turned out.

Her Mama clinks the glasses in the kitchen. Egg tries to think about Albert's story. There doesn't seem to be a moral except Stay Off the Train Tracks and You Won't Be Hit and Flung into the River. You can only have a moral at the very end. That's when you know how the story turns out.

Egg looks down at her paper. There are so many ideas but they are all jumbled up in her brain. Her notebook helps. Anne Frank wrote down all her thoughts in her diary and she made it into her best friend, Kitty. She put up posters of her favourite film stars in the Secret Annex and made family trees of People in History. She even read books of folks Egg has never heard of—all to make sense of what was happening to her and her family.

Egg bites her lip. If her life were a story, what would she write?

Once upon a time
There was a family
With ostriches
They were Japanese

Not the ostriches.

Egg pauses. She thinks, people die all the time. You make up a story to make sense of the world. But what if the world doesn't make sense?

No no no. The world must make sense. Like Our Father who Art in Heaven. Like Character is Destiny. There must be some kind of clue, some kind of sign. Yes, there must be. She just needs more facts. Like a scientist. Like a detective.

Egg stares down at the page. Stories are harder than they seem. She flips over the sheet and begins to write *I promise to be good* over and over again, filling the lines with her scrawl. It is her pact with the world. She knows that it only comes true if you believe it. It only becomes real when you write it down.

. . .

Egg crouches in the shadows of the kitchen table. It's like the *Mutual of Omaha's Wild Kingdom* — the cheetahs and the leopards on the Vast Open Plains of the Serengeti. Egg likes the part about the mama cheetahs romping with her cubs in the tall grasses, climbing into the low spreading, branching arms of the acacia trees. The papa cheetahs are nowhere to be found. That's just the way it is. Egg looks away at the stalking, at the poor gazelles and impalas, but she knows the facts of life. Here, beneath the kitchen table, as Egg weaves her body around the legs of the kitchen chairs, it is like playing hide-and-seek with herself but tonight she is watching Mama. It's like the empirical method that way. Mama, with her bluebird apron, the steam fogging the window, the click-clack of forks and spoons settling in the big sink, the splosh of dishes as Mama submerges them in the sudsy water.

Mama's thick black hair is cut to a no-nonsense bob. Her bangs fall over her eyes as she leans over the sink and scrubs the big pot. *Scratch scratch scratch* — Egg doesn't like the sound of the bristle brush. The grey at Mama's temples came after Albert's accident. Mama's hair was once as long and as thick as a rope, just like a fairy tale Rapunzel, a once upon a time of sleepy tuck-ins, of good nights, of Mama's long, black strands flowing through Egg's fingers, like water, like wind.

After Albert's funeral Mama cut her hair so that's the end of that.

Mama wipes her hands on the apron. Mama's hands always surprise Egg. They are swift and delicate, flitting like a small bird.

"Careful of your head, little one," Mama says without turning.

Egg jerks up — her forehead smashes on the bottom of the chair. She catches the whimper in her teeth.

"What are you doing down there?" Mama asks. She turns from the dishes, the bubbles still clinging to her fingers, and sits by the kitchen table. "Let me see that," she coaxes, sliding Egg onto her lap. She pushes back Egg's hair, to reveal the bump on her forehead. "You've got an egg-bump," Mama says playfully and kisses the small welt lightly.

"I'm all right," Egg sniffs, blinking away her tears.

Mama strokes back Egg's tumbled hair, looping a strand behind her ears. "You're a Murakami. A stoic through and through."

"What's a stoic?"

Mama purses her lips. She slips her hand into her apron pocket and pops a mint into Egg's mouth. A melty mint, white on the outside, green on the inside. Egg's favourite.

"How come you don't talk like Papa?"

Her mother raises her eyebrows. "What do you mean?"

"He doesn't really talk like Hop Sing on *Ponderosa* but he doesn't talk like you either."

"That's because Papa was born in Japan and I was born in Vancouver."

"How did you meet him?"

"In Japan. After the war."

Egg clicks her tongue against her front teeth to get all of the minty goodness. "How come you were in Japan?" She doesn't want to ask about the war thing.

Mama gazes at her and Egg can feel her hesitation. Mama says, "I got lost in the shuffle." She follows up briskly with, "And your father, he just swept me off my feet. I mean, really — he was on a motorcycle and he almost ran me over. But he made up for that later with chocolates and nylons." She leans in conspiratorially, "I think he pinched them from the American base where he was working. And his hair!" Mama juts out her chin and swoops her hand over her forehead, "Swept up like Elvis."

Egg laughs, trying to imagine her father's hips swinging to "Jailhouse Rock."

Mama sighs. "He was so crazy about baseball. He wanted to be pitcher for the New York Yankees." Her smile dwindles. "Imagine that." Her eyes dart to the window.

"Mama?"

Mama blinks. She looks down at Egg. "All better?" she asks.

Egg nods.

Mama rises, sliding Egg from her lap. "You go play now."

"But I can help," Egg says. She doesn't want to leave her Mama, not yet. Quickly, she drags the kitchen chair to the counter where the dish rack sits. She pulls the towel from the oven handle and steps onto the chair. Egg totters for a moment but her Mama's hand braces her, there, on the small of her back.

They stand eye to eye.

Egg's mother gazes at her. Egg stares. Her mother's eyes are a rich, deep brown, ringed with fine lines. She looks sad and tired. For a moment, Egg wonders if she has done anything wrong. She wonders what Albert would have said.

The steam rises, glowing against the foggy window. The groan of the barn gate echoes across the yard. Egg waits for the throaty call of the ostriches, their *Woooh woooh wooooh*. Do they ever get lonely? The square glow of her father's window shimmers like a beacon in the dark.

Her mother's arm reaches around Egg, pulls her close. Egg wants to ask, but she doesn't know the question. She thinks of the cheetahs on the Serengeti, the survival of the fittest, the good and the bad and the Moral of the Story. Rapunzel, locked in the tower, but what bad did she do? Her father stole from the witch but why was she the one who was punished?

"You can help," Mama says. "Can you get the dinner tin from Papa?"

Egg feels the heaviness in her chest. She wants to hold onto the warmth of the kitchen but she looks out to the barn. A shiver snakes through her belly but she quells it. She can be brave. She can do it for her Mama. With one hop, she is off the chair and halfway to the porch.

The door slams behind her.

Wooh-wooh-woooohhh.

Run run run as fast as you can, you can't catch me, I'm the gingerbread man. The field is a blur but Egg is already at the gate, pushing it open.

"Papa," she pants.

Papa does not seem surprised at her sudden appearance. He holds the steaming kettle and pours the water into three shallow pans on the wood stove. A hiss as the water sputters and bubbles. The steam rises to the shadows of the beams.

"I came to pick up your tin," she says.

He gestures for her to come closer as he walks to the work table. "I have something for you." He takes the egg on the setting tray, the one that has been waiting.

Egg stands beside him.

Her father holds the egg against his chest, as if feeling for any vibrations. He cups the cream-white shell in his hand, as if measuring its strength. He places his ear against the porous calcite. He nods and eases the orb into Egg's hands. She feels the shell, that paradoxical mix of cool porcelain and warm interior. The weight calms her, she holds a thrill of anticipation, of something magical and alive. Egg can hear a faint chirp from the egg—the chick has pierced the air sac but still the surface of the egg is unbroken. If the chick does not break through, it will suffocate in its shell.

Egg feels a tremor, a peck, but the chick, still pipping, has not torn through the membrane.

She looks at Papa. "It's still alive."

Her father takes the egg and places it into the hatch box, his fingers grazing along the sides of the oval as the egg finds its balance. He pulls out the white bottle of rubbing alcohol and a pad of cotton batten from the box beside the hatch crate. From his tool box he takes the drill and drops the smallest bit into the chuck, tightens it, and gives it an exploratory whirl. He cups the egg and runs his thumb along the crown to the base, where the air sac would be. Cautiously, he lays the drill bit almost parallel to the hard surface, working a groove into the glossy shell. She knows he is too careful for a puncture. A fine dust clouds the air and tiny shards fly off, the grit of ceramic. At breaking point he puts down the drill and dabs his fingers onto the alcohol swabs, his fingertips stark against the chalk dust. He presses through the alabastrine cover with the tip of his index finger and gently peels back the opaque membrane.

Egg can see the slick, tiny head of the chick, the bulbous eyes.

The beak moves. *Chirp.*

Papa places the egg into the hatch box, beneath the strong heat of the overhead lamp. Egg knows that he will do no more. The chick must find its own way out of the vessel. As he gathers the fine china shards, Egg reflects on her father. The lines in his face have deepened, as if the years have cut sharp, almost to the bone. She knows that he could help the chick, he could, but he has told her that only the strong survive.

She cannot ask him to come back to the house (is that why her mother has sent her here?) for a wordless part of her knows that the barn is his test, his trial, his sacrifice. Egg has her questions but they shrivel and harden, as if into stone. Beside her father, she cannot ask the whys or the hows and so she swallows them. As they stand, her small fingers slip into his chalky hand. They watch the chick, its struggle, for it is the struggle that makes you stronger.

. . .

Later that night, when Egg creeps down the stairs in her slippery socks, she sees Mama in the living room, slumped in the big chair. The television is on the late night show of *Onward Christian Soldiers*. A pledge of ten dollars a month gets you a Bible with a golden pin. The choir, all dressed in white, sings with an unearthly fervour "Are You Washed in the Blood?" but Mama does not stir. The electronic glow of the screen bathes her in a ghastly pallor. Dead dead dead and Egg almost screams.

"Egg, go upstairs." Kathy's voice comes from behind her. Kathy's hand is on her Mama's shoulder, jostling her.

"She's not dead, is she?"

"No," Kathy says, with a glance at the bottle on the coffee table. "She just . . . here, could you turn off the television?"

Egg clicks off the set. She can smell the acrid liquor, like the clinging scent of gasoline.

"I want to help."

"Go to bed, Egg. You'll just be in the way." Kathy leans forward. With a deep breath, she loops her mother's arm around her shoulders and lifts her to her feet. Kathy eases her Mama up the stairs, the creak and stagger, the scrape along the wall, the groan of the mattress springs as Kathy rolls her mother into her bed.

As Egg hovers by Mama's doorway, she realizes Kathy has done this all before. A queasiness shifts in the pit of her stomach.

Kathy pulls up the covers. Mama's eyes flutter open.

Dark. Mama's eyes are dark. "You're such a good girl." Her voice is whiskey gravel, so quiet, so heavy in the shadows of the room. "When I was your age—"

"Shh, Mama."

Mama sighs, skipping stones through her memories. She swirls in a spiral of whiskey and mints. "What was that song? A Lullaby, a "Lullaby in Birdland." He used to like that. American Jazz."

But Albert liked *Soul Train* and *American Bandstand*.

"They take them away. They always take the good ones away."

Egg backs out of the room, her legs rubbery. She runs down the hall and jumps into her bed, twisting the blankets around her. The good ones. The ones her Mama loves the best.

Egg burrows deeper.

Head tucked in, she hears the click of the lamp and even in the cocoon of blankets, the world glows golden.

Egg pops her head out.

"Hey." Kathy sits at the edge of the bed. The crease between her eyebrows has deepened. "You all right?"

Egg nods.

"She's going to be fine. She's not going to die."

"Everyone dies, you know." Egg tries to make this a matter of fact.

Kathy tucks the blanket around her. "Do you remember when you were four years old, you started crying at the table, right out of nowhere, and when we asked you why, you said, 'I'll be lonely when everyone dies.'"

"But I am the youngest and I'm going to die last."

Kathy opens her mouth but can only puff out her cheeks. "Why do you think of such big questions?"

"All the small ones lead to big ones."

Kathy picks up Nekoneko who has fallen from the bed. "Do you want me to read a little bit of the book?" Kathy taps the paperback on the bedside table, a copy of *Anne Frank: Diary of a Young Girl.*

Egg nods again.

"Then scoot over."

Kathy crawls into the cramped space beside her sister. Egg nestles in, closing her eyes, her head on Kathy's shoulder. "Now let's see," Kathy says as she flips through the pages. Egg can hear the words, feel them, a rumble through Kathy's chest.

Kathy begins:

"Dear Diary. It's been a while since I've written but we've finally made the journey to America. So much has happened since our escape by train, since our long voyage across the ocean. Mother ate so much fish and cabbage on the ship that she threw up before we could dock. We're settling in though. We've started school and Margot is surrounded by so many beaux. Peter is so behind in his studies and all he thinks about is the war but Father says there's time enough for that. Father seems a little lost somehow, maybe because of all the changes. It is hard to be tossed from our cozy Secret Annex but what a relief it is to be out of that cage. Safe and without worry. I do wonder about the world though. What will happen? What will the future bring?"

Kathy shifts. Egg wills her breathing into an even flow, pretending to sleep. Kathy slowly eases her way out of the bed and clicks off the bedside lamp. In the dark, Egg measures the day. She tries to think of Elvis, of motorcycles, and melty mints. She knows that Good Mama is gone in a whiskey swirl, lost in the shuffle.

· · ·

It is Sunday and from the pulpit Reverend Samuels crows about damnation and the everlasting love of the Prince of Peace. Egg perches on the edge of her seat and tries to make sense of it all. Jesus crucified on the hills of Calgary. But if God created the world in seven days, where did the Devil come from? She squirms on the hard wooden pew. Kathy, beside her, taps on the hymn book and hums "Born to be Wild." Her mother nods and sways at every amen. The veins are popping out of Reverend Samuels's forehead as he strains for the passion. He is going to pop a gasket.

Those are her Papa's words — pop a gasket. He says might as well pray to a tube of toothpaste: cavities are the real evil.

It is like Papa has cut himself off from the world. If he doesn't believe then he is going to Hell. And how can it be Heaven if all those you love aren't there?

But here, in the brightly lit nave of Bittercreek United Church, Egg is surrounded by Hosannas and Hallelujahs, the gasps and sighs of the faithful. It is hard to figure everything out. She looks around her, at the good citizens of her small town. What do they believe in? That Goodness is rewarded and Badness is punished? And can you be Good but do Bad?

What does that make you? Reverend Samuels says the Wages of Sin is Death but doesn't everybody die anyway? And Mama, what is she looking for in the vaulted ceiling and stained glass? What does she pray for?

From her seat at the back, Egg can see a good chunk of Bittercreek, the thinning heads and comb-overs, home perms from Julie Duncan's kitchen, the crewcuts from Nelson's Barber Shop down on Maple. There are no long-haired hippies in Bittercreek, that is only on television, like on *The Mod Squad*. But as Egg looks up at the cross, she realizes that Jesus looks like a long-haired hippie.

In the basement of Bittercreek United Church, surrounded by a mural of Jesus healing the Leapers, in Mrs. MacDonnell's Junior Sunday School class, Egg raises her hand.

Answers. She needs some answers.

Mrs. MacDonnell's nose twitches.

"Yes, Egg?"

"If Jesus died so we can be saved...why did He have to die so we can be saved?"

"So His blood can wash away our sins." Mrs. MacDonnell speaks slowly, each word a biting clip.

"But couldn't He do that anyway, being God and all?"

Mrs. MacDonnell's ears blush pink. "It was His plan. We cannot presume to know The Ways of God."

Egg sits, stumped. The Ways of God argument. There is no way around that one.

"But if we were made in God's image..." Egg thinks of Mama and her whiskey. "Why do we need to be saved?"

Mrs. MacDonnell twitches. Her eyes bulge like the classroom goldfish. "Sin entered the world when we ate of the Tree of Knowledge and for that all of mankind is tainted," she says finally.

"But didn't God put it there? I mean, it sounds like a trick to me, like the three wishes that make everything worse."

Mrs. MacDonnell burns red. "Out!" she shouts, as if to expel Satan himself. Egg still has questions about Mama and the Wine in Cana, about Papa in the ostrich barn—she just wants to know how to save them, for they are lost, lost in their own desert, their own wandering wilderness. The Devil is out there, she knows it, but Mrs. MacDonnell's finger calls down the Wrath of Righteousness and it is out the door for her.

> *Our Father, whose Art in Heaven,*
> *hollow be thy name;*
> *thy kingdom come,*
> *thy will be done*
> *on Earth as it is in Heaven.*
> *Give us this day,*
> *our daily bread*
> *and forgive us our trespasses,*
> *as we forgive those who trespass against us*
> *and lead us not onto the Temptations*
> *but deliver us from evil.*
> *For thine is the kingdom,*
> *for power and for glory,*
> *forever and never.*
> *Amen.*

And so Egg, banished from the doors of Mrs. MacDonnell's Sunday school class, her head bowed against the heavy hand of God, whispers a prayer for the lost souls who have turned away from Jesus who loves the little children, all the children of the world. But then she thinks of all the little ones who have not heard the Word and she shivers. She knows that there are places without Jesus and radios and *Gilligan's Island*. Hellfire burns hot and eternal and forever is a long, long time. Deep in the darkest depths of her soul, Egg knows that something is wrong, very wrong, wronger than all the burning barns and bloody lambs in all the Bibles, in all the world, so that when the church bell rings and Martin Fisken finally comes and hits her, she is almost happy.

. . .

In the kitchen, Egg opens the cupboards, peers into the corners, behind the boxes and bins. The days have tumbled by and Egg still does not have any answers. It seems like she can't even get the questions right. If she were smarter, and older, she would know what to do. She needs the bigger picture, the Moral of the Story. Yesterday she found the magnifying glass in her father's tool box along with a cat's eye marble. She promises herself that she will put it back. It's not stealing if you put it back.

If you hold a marble up in the air, you can see the world shift through different colours. Everything changes, Egg thinks. Newton will tell you that.

Mama's Jack Daniel's hides behind the flour bin. Egg sloshes the half-bottle in her hand. She knows that whiskey makes her Mama blurry. She holds up the bottle against the late afternoon light and peers into the liquid that looks like the last moment of sunset, a deep summer honey that has mellowed into autumn. Carefully, she tops it up with water. She stares at the bottle.

This is what makes Mama Not-Mama. This grown-up stuff, like cigarettes, like S - E - X. Egg brings the bottle close and wrinkles her nose against the sour. Quickly, she takes a sip. Poison! She spits out the burn. Without a second thought, she dumps the bottle into the sink and watches the amber swirl away from her.

Now she's done it.

The bottle is empty.

For a second she thinks of putting maple syrup into the bottle but Mama would know because of the taste. Then she thinks of her secret hiding place: the loft. Egg must get rid of the evidence. Bottle tucked under her armpit, she runs to the side of the barn, to the ladder by the side shed. Up she goes, to the creaking roof of the shed. The splinters prick against her knees and elbows as she makes her way across the slanting overhang, into the small window of the barn's loft. She closes the shutter behind her.

She has stashed her comics here, in the darkness of the barn above the ostriches. Albert's blanket, the one she has pinched from the boxes below, makes a cozy berth. A wooden crate holds her comics and clippings of her favourite TV shows, along with odds and ends: Botan candy toys from Nakashima's in Lethbridge, a pin of the USS *Uganda* that she found on Centre Street in Calgary. Her Evel Knievel doll, the one she bought at the Stampede, sits coldly observing from his ledge. And here, a stack of her precious *TV Guides*, a rarity in Bittercreek—she can look up *The Streets of San Francisco* even if Kathy won't let her watch it. She places Mama's bottle beside the crate and jams her candle stub in the stopper. Here, above the restless ostriches, she flips through her superhero comics: secret identities and double lives. In the back pages of the comics there are miracles—Johnny Altas transformed from a ninety-pound weakling, Kung Fu Secrets Revealed, Learn Hypnotism, and Rubber Masks that are Amazingly Real! The X-ray glasses are the best—Egg wants them more than anything else in the world. X-ray, like a superhero. Egg knows that only a few letters set invisibility from invincibility: that must be a sign.

Her father scrapes the shovel in the pens below her, a syncopated *shh-shh, shh-shh* that is unexpectedly comforting. Egg presses her nose against the floorboards and peers through the gap in the slats. But he is only a sliver here, so she scoots near the crate, to the hole in the wood, her special eye-knot, spy-knot.

He is right below her. Egg thinks that he looks flat, like all the gravity has pressed him down but she knows the word for this—perspective. His hair falls, uneven, as if he had hacked blindly at his head. Egg remembers her Papa before he moved into the ostrich barn, his hair, so black, the cut, precise. Now, it's like he is undone. Papa is unravelling.

Chirp chirp, from the crate. He has lengthened the run and there is new chicken wire along the bottom of the last pen. The hatchlings have grown into chicks, their dun-coloured feathers still short and stiff. Some chicks have twine looped around their splaying knees—her father's own remedy for the ones who have trouble walking on the jute.

With a click of the gate latch, her father goes through the grill to the outside pens. Egg runs to the corner of the loft, to the creaking ladder that leads down to the boxes. Cautiously, with foot to foot and hand to hand, she descends. Ladders always feel like the edge of the world.

She rummages through Albert's suitcase that holds his ties, his best shoes, and his jangles and jingles—pins, a watch, an old key chain of Tetsuwan Atom. She has his set of Disappearing Cups but she wants real magic, not some sleight of hand. Those are tricks and tricks are not fair.

She picks up Albert's silver dollar and tries to do his knuckle roll but the silver glints and slips through her fingers. The coin rolls in a spiral loop, into the chick's pen.

Damn, she swears in a grown-up way. Damn.

Her father is still raking the outside pens. If she cranes her neck far enough, she can see him through the grill.

Plan A, Egg thinks. She grabs a handful of feed pellets.

She slides to the door of the chick pen, making herself as small as possible. She opens the latch and squeezes herself inside. Quiet, quiet, she tells herself but it is too late—the chicks run towards her, cheeping, flapping, their excitement mounting. Egg will be overrun soon so she flings the feed pellets to the back of the pen and laughs as the chicks dart madly after the bait. She picks up Albert's silver dollar and pockets it.

Pluck. She feels a pluck at her elbow. A chick, smaller than the rest of the brood, no more than a ball of fuzz and a twitchy head, topples at her side. Its feet scrabble against the jute. The head, held up by a noodle neck, bobs, insistent. Its beak opens with a squawk, calling the other fledglings who rush over, trampling it.

Egg reaches out for the fallen chick and remembers her father's instruction—scoop from below, her arm to cradle, not to crush, her hand to support. The chick is the smallest, the slowest one, the one whose pipping had not broken through. A runt, like Wilbur in *Charlotte's Web*, an underdog. Egg holds it loose yet not too loose. Like the Goldilocks story, she does it just right. She runs her fingers through the soft brown feathers, over its downy fuzz-covered head. Its eyes are luminous, magically liquid, magically light. Egg shivers at the chick's fragility. Holding its skittery body, wiggling head, and jutting legs dangling ridiculously, she can feel its beating heart, right in the palm of her hand.

This one she will call Esmeralda.

. . .

Today is a *D* day. *D* days start off wrong—like don't and dumb and doorknob. *D* days and Mama can't get up from bed and Kathy is a grouch. *D* is dead and damn and dump and ditch.

D day and Egg must be careful. She rubs the outline of Albert's silver dollar stashed safely in her pocket. At least she has a plan.

In the science room, the glass display holds the skeletons of prairie dogs and field mice. A stuffed fox, with a red-devil grin, stands above the chemistry cabinets with the sign: "Danger. Mixing Explosives May Be Harmful To Your Health." In the science room, the granite floor is a cold, speckled grey. On the long side-counter there are lines and lines of Bunsen burners and test tubes. Jars and jars of impaled and drowning potatoes clutter the shelf by the window. It hurts Egg's eyes just to look at them. Potatoes have eyes. She tries not to think of this.

This is the most dangerous time for Egg, the second half of lunch break. Martin Fisken, along with the rest of the townies, is back from his house, after *The Buck Shot Show*. With the rain, all the students are corralled in the halls and the common rooms. Students sit at the tables, textbooks open.

Today, Egg will try the science room. Martin has spotted her in the library too many times before.

The science room sparkles with a crisp, clean glamour. It's all falling stars and comet tails, prism rainbows with a Reach for the Future poster that reminds her of the Jetsons. A model of the Solar System dangles from the ceiling with icy Pluto banished to the corner. Jupiter is the Roman name for Zeus, the Greek God of Thunder. Jupiter has a spot. At the centre of the science room, the Earth spins. A segment slides out to reveal a pie-cut of crust, mantle, and core.

Science is the very big and the very small. The glass cases of butterflies pinned to the whiteboard. The jewel eyes of dragon-flies. The gossamer wings of cicadas.

Egg bows her head over these tiny crucifixions. They are the Jesuses of the insect world, a sacrifice for science. Troubled, she turns away.

Egg wants something solid, not this crash and bang of plates and shifts and continental drifts. In the science room, a model of the volcano smoulders in the corner. Egg knows that volcanoes, like dinosaurs, can go extinct, but she has seen the pictures of Pompeii. The science room is not at all like the library. Science strips and bares but the library builds on words, like an *abracadabra* that becomes an adventure. Egg has read the *Young Reader's Guide to Science* but that is more like a story: Galileo recanting in the face of the Inquisition. But Galileo won after all because science is like that. Facts are not lies. Facts win out in the end. It bothers Egg though, how could the Bible be wrong? She will have to ask Mrs. MacDonnell about that. Mrs. MacDonnell does not like questions. Anything less than blind faith makes a heretic and heretics burn. There is the black and white of it but Egg doesn't understand; there is black and white and good and evil—but where does the Japanese fit in?

Did Galileo burn?

Egg picks her way through the chrome taps and microscopes, weaving her way through the crowd. At least with so many people about, it is easier to hide. She skulks by the beaker cabinet then dashes by the dinosaur dino-rama. A crowd of Mr. Gooch's keeners heads her way so Egg crawls underneath the film strip table. Camouflage, like on the *Mutual of Omaha's Wild Kingdom*.

The bottom of the table holds an impressive array of chewing gum, wads of pink Bubble-Deelight and green smears of Minty Freeze. Rumour is that Bubble-Deelight is filled with spiders' eggs so Egg scoots deeper, far from the edge. Spiders have eight legs so they are not insects. Egg knows there are rules for everything. With the *Young Reader's Guide to Science*, Egg can tell you about the planets and the constellations and sometimes, at night, she can look out of her window and see Orion's Belt. The universe is vast, this she knows. The Big Bang is so huge, you can't even imagine it and the speed of light is the fastest thing ever.

"Has anyone seen that stupid Egghead?" Martin's voice rings out.

Egg freezes. She can see Martin Fisken's sneakers by the dino-rama but she is safe under the film strip table. When she peeps at the clock above the door, she knows that there are thirty more minutes until the bell rings. An eternity.

She hugs her knees and begins her list:

a – armadillo
b – baboon
c – crocodile
d – dugong
e – elephant
f – flamingo
g – giraffe
h – hippopotamus
i – ibis
j – jellyfish
k – kangaroo
l – llama
m – monkey
n –
none
never
no
n n n n n n n n

There is no Dictionary beneath the table. Egg is stuck. *Nnnnn* on her tongue. Few animals start with the letter *n*. *N* is a tricky one: knolls, knots, and gnarls try to hide the *n* away. *Nnnnn*. She counts the passing penny loafers and sneakers, but the *nnnn* presses anxiously against her throat.

The Dictionary has the answers.

She darts from beneath the table, away from the fossilized bones of the science room, the whiteboard displays of genus and species. She rushes along the corridor, under the harsh fluorescent lights of the hallway, past the lunchroom. The staccato notes from the music room echo behind her, until at last, she reaches the library. She slips through the swing of the doors and ducks under the sight of Miss Granger, who, distracted by her Dewey decimals, does not see her shadow flit into the aisle of Afghanistan. Egg's fingers brush the spines of the books as she tiptoes to Upper Volta.

She taps her feet. Everything will be all right.

A crackle fills the air. Evangeline Granger has turned on the radio to the lulling tones of the midday CBC. Now Egg knows that the library is really empty for the radio is Miss Granger's secret indulgence. Home free, Egg sighs, but the words seem hollow.

After an blurt of static, the CBC announces the next segment of "Babbino" and "Callas," but Egg pays it no mind. Her thoughts are all about how to avoid Martin Fisken and his gang but the voice from the radio catches her—a voice that sings and soars and Egg must listen. She holds the notes like a flutter in her chest, a sudden fullness that she can barely contain; she feels prickles behind her ears, a chill on the back of her neck. The song rises and falls like a wind that cradles and caresses. She thinks of mermaids singing, of whales calling in the deep, even the ostriches *wooh-wooh-wooohhh*.

A song to wash out all the bad in the world.

A song to make it all better.

Egg pushes the book cart aside and peers out between the gap in the book stand. Behind the counter, Evangeline Granger is frozen, her cheeks blanching, like a watercolour left out in the rain. Egg's throat clutches as she watches Evangeline's tears. She knows she should not be a witness to this but she must do something. The song, so like a spell, has cast Evangeline into her private sorrow. Egg must free Evangeline, so much like a fairy tale princess. Evangeline, who gives her lollipops on bad days.

Egg thinks of Mama's mints that she has borrowed. She has stowed them carefully in her coat pocket. That is something, a small comfort she can give. A thunderbolt hits her — it's a chance for her to be a Hero! Without a second thought, she dashes towards her classroom.

Egg pokes her head through the doorway. Her classroom is empty. It seems smaller with everyone gone. She spies her coat hanging on the hook at the back of the class and runs to it. Her fingers scrabble for the mints at the bottom of her inside pocket. She clutches them in her palm, the white powder floating in the air, that smell of freshness, of green.

Yes, this is perfect.

A hand grabs hold of her throat and she is thrown against the wall. The mints tumble from her hand.

Egg can hear the crunch of the candy beneath Martin Fisken's feet. Behind him, Chuckie and Brendan sneer.

"Wait," Egg shouts, and roots in her pocket. She pulls out Albert's silver dollar and holds it out to Martin so that it catches the light. Her plan. She feels her heels touch the floor as he takes the coin and releases her.

"Wow," Chuckie says, "that's a real silver dollar."

Martin slides it into his pocket. Egg's shoulders fall with relief. But Martin's hand smashes into her chest. The silver dollar — there is not even time enough for unfair — the wind is knocked out of her.

Martin smiles. Egg can see his tooth, the pointed one as he grins tightly, like a fox, like a devil.

. . .

Egg is cold. She is wet. She is blind.

She doesn't like these things. She can't get out. It's dark and it's like forever.

. . .

After an eternity, the locker opens and Kathy is there. The light is such a relief, as Kathy rubs the warmth back into Egg's shaking arms. Kathy wraps up Egg's bleeding knuckles with her handkerchief. Kathy's look, so full of pity, so full of rage but Egg can still hear the silent admonishment, something like *Oh, Egg*...

"I'm sorry Kathy."

Couldn't you fit in for once in your life?

Kathy wraps her jacket around Egg and holds her. "It's all right, sweetie." But her gentleness is too much, all of Egg's fear, locked and twisted in the dark, releases in a sob as Kathy holds her, rocking, just holds her.

. . .

Boom, swoosh, boom. Egg must run to keep up with Kathy's stride, as they cross the schoolyard. Kathy seems like a force of nature, a whirlwind of energy. Egg can't keep her eyes off her, the muscle twitching in her jaw, the scanning gaze, that dagger focus. She thinks Kathy needs a thunderbolt, or wings that can span her fury. By the jungle gym Kathy swoops in, three quick strides and she has Martin Fisken by the collar, his feet barely touching the ground.

Kathy's voice is low and steady. "Now what did I say about staying away from my little sister?"

(71)

Martin can barely stutter before Kathy grabs his back and yanks his underwear, lifting him off the ground for an astral wedgie. He screams, his eyes bulging. Kathy pulls him up to the jungle gym hook by his underwear and leaves him to hang. Kathy's hand pats Egg's shoulder as the other kids look on in awe and amazement.

Egg glances back at her wonderstruck classmates, up at her looming sister. Kathy looks a thousand feet tall. Egg trots to keep up with her long stride. As they approach the doors, she slips her hand into Kathy's palm and feels the answering squeeze.

Kathy, with a grudging smile, tells her, "It'll be okay. I promise, Egg."

She promises.

. . .

In bed, Egg pulls the blanket over her head as Mama and Kathy yell in the kitchen, Mama calling up Jesus to turn the other cheek and Kathy shouting to Hell with all of that. Egg bites her hand. Hell. H E double hockey sticks. Her knuckles still bleed from the inside of the locker. Kathy has gotten a week's detention for stringing up Martin Fisken but she just shrugs it off. How can she be so brave? Now Mama is saying she doesn't like Kathy's attitude, how she dresses, or how she hangs out with Stacey Norman and, last of all, how Mama's whiskey has gone missing.

Egg curls deeper under her covers.

It is her fault. Reverend Samuels always says that things happen for a reason. It is her fault for Mama and Kathy screaming at each other, Papa in the ostrich barn, and Albert in Heaven.

And she has lost the silver dollar. Albert's silver dollar. Her plan was a complete failure. She takes out her notebook and writes:

Not Fair! Not Fair!

She scribbles a circle on the page. Round and round in frustration, until the pencil gouges into the paper, round and round until the tip breaks. Stab, stab, stab, into the centre.

Egg stares at the hole on the page. She will not cry. She places her forehead against the notebook.

Sorry. Sorry. Sorry.

Her tears blot the sheet. With her eyes full of tears, her fingers fumble for the broken head of the pencil. With the stub of lead, she writes:

Money did not work with Martin.
Plan did not work.
The hurt is what he is after.

. . .

She slides off the bed, imagining some kind of abyss, or chasm. The edge of the world, the end of it. She wants to plummet and shatter, the whole day broken, her whole life wrong. She falls, eyes closed, feels the vertiginous drop, that spike of fear. Her back hits the floor, a bump on the back of her head. There. With a slow roll, she scoots under the bed.

Egg clutches *Anne Frank: Diary of a Young Girl* and the *Young Reader's Guide to Science.* She wants to know how to survive the worst things. Her eyes are blurry but she tells no one. She can't read the blackboard and Mrs. Syms thinks she is stupid, but a four-eyes ostrich Egghead is just too much in Bittercreek, the laws of nature would not allow it. Egg squints and tries to read about Newton and the apples and the oranges in the *Young Reader's Guide to Science.* There is no equal opposite force at rest or in motion. This is the law of everything. Egg yawns. She gazes at the photograph of Anne Frank at the back of the book and rubs stars into her eyes. There is a secret, some kind of code that will make everything better. She has looked around and everyone seems to know it, some kind of key, or sign, or something. In the beginning was the Word and the end will be Revelation. If she stares long enough at the photo, Anne Frank will tell her. Egg is patient. Good things come to those who wait.

Wonder Woman has magical bracelets that deflect bullets and she carries the Lasso of Truth. But you can see her through her invisible plane, sitting upright and everything in her golden wonder bra all in the middle of the air. Egg wants to be a superhero but not like Wonder Woman. Every superhero has a fatal flaw that the Greeks call hubris. Pride is what the lions have, on their golden fields of Savannah. *Mutual of Omaha* tells us so. The king of the beasts, they tell us, but if there are kings, then there are queens and knights and sacrificial pawns and pride that goes before the Fall.

As Egg hears Kathy stamp up the stairs, she grabs her blue Ninny Blankie from the top of the bed and scuttles underneath again. Her door gives a creak as it opens. Egg can see her sister's scuffed up sneakers—and then Kathy's head after she drops to her knees and looks under the bed.

"Come on, Egg," Kathy says, "let's get out of here."

. . .

Kathy drives the truck down the trail as Egg bounces on the seat beside her. With the windows rolled down, Egg feels the wind through her hair, the roar in her ears. On this gravel strip, the rocks spray upwards, flung from the roll of the tires, ringing a metallic melody of pings and rattles. To the west, the foothills rise over the late autumn evening, as the sky rolls with clouds, a fistful of sunlight punching through. Distance is a smear on the horizon.

The dusk floats down, flattening the fields for as far as the eye can see.

They are going to the coulee.

Egg feels the descent before she sees it, the truck speeding faster. The silver glint of sage sparkles on the slope with a burst of yellow cactus flowers amidst the crop of prickles. It always surprises Egg, this rift in the plain, the sudden drop. As they descend, the horizon rises and the sun flashes in the grooves of the ridge—then a darkness as the coulee swallows them. Kathy clicks on her headlights.

"Woooo," Egg howls, as the bump at the bottom of the trail jolts her out of her seat and she sails off the vinyl, floating for a moment in the cab of the truck. Every speck on the windshield, every scratch on the dash seems vital, important. The dangling green Little Tree on the rear-view mirror, the glint of Kathy's key chain with her peace sign pendant. Egg can see the smallest detail. There is the faint scent of day-old skunk wafting from the roadside, mixing with the synthetic pine. Her skin tingles. She feels the lift, the air surrounds her—she is free.

Egg is defying gravity.

"—ooo!" She lands hard on the edge of the weathered vinyl, a small bounce as the spring jabs against her tailbone.

She winces but the flight is worth it.

Kathy cranks up the radio against the din of gravel. The uneven trail rocks them from side to side. Cat Stevens on the dial, with the strum of his guitar. Kathy and Egg begin to sing "Oh Very Young," away from the house, the barn, the town. They skid across what was once a riverbed to the bottom of the coulee. Egg wonders why the song is so sad when they are so very young. It is a sweet kind of sadness that melts on your tongue and lingers.

At the foot of the coulee Kathy parks the truck beneath the spread of mottled cottonwoods. Kathy slams the door behind her with a satisfying thud. Egg scrambles towards the firepit, her foot catching on a raised root.

"Help me get some kindling," Kathy hollers. As an after-thought she adds, "But don't go too far."

Beneath the cottonwoods, Egg gathers twigs and, cautiously in the crook of her arm, brittle thistles. She pulls at a sprig of sage. Her feet rustle through the carpet of diamond-shaped leaves. At the tallest tree, she places her hand on the thick, fissured bark. She winds through the trunks, to the stand of white spruce. She picks up the slender cones, her feet crunching through the leaves to the mouldy damp below.

Kathy stacks a loose pyramid of deadfall branches in the firepit and scatters Egg's tinder inside. She shifts the logs, push-ing them further from the pit. Egg watches as Kathy lights the kindling—the flash as the match head strikes the side of the Redbird box—and blows the embers into a smoky spiral. In the fire, the nettles crackle, the snap-spark as the burrs curl against the heat, succumbing to the flame. Egg rubs the grit off her palms, the slight indent of needle and pine. Her hands hold the scent of sage. She sits on the log, hands to the fire as she wiggles her fingers against the dancing light.

Kathy slaps her hands together, brushing off the dirt. She hunkers down next to Egg.

"Egg?"

"Hm?"

"What did you do with the whiskey?"

Egg hugs her fists to her chest. So this is why Kathy has brought her here, away from the house, away from Mama. "I poured it down the drain," she peeps.

Kathy sighs. "Well, at least you didn't drink it." Her voice is caught between relief and exasperation.

"No, it's nasty." Egg looks down at her feet.

Kathy throws the spruce cones into the fire. They give a good spark. She says, "You have to think of Mama like she's sick."

"When is she going to get better?"

"Soon." But Egg can see that Kathy is gazing into the dark of the woods, nodding her head, as if she is trying to convince herself.

Egg bites her lip. "Is it because of Albert?"

"Yes...and no. You'll understand when you get older."

Egg is about to ask another why but she sees her sister's face, the line between Kathy's eyebrows that deepens when she is troubled. Albert never had that line. Kathy was the serious one, the one who buys the groceries at Gustafsson's and flushes out the ostrich puke that sinks to the bottom of the trough. Last year it was Kathy who came in for Egg's Parent-Teacher Interview. She had convinced Mrs. Figgis not to hold Egg back with the first-year runts.

Kathy turns up her collar and pats her pockets for her cigarettes. Her face is lit in the glow of her lighter, cupped in her hands as she shields the flame.

It isn't fair, Egg thinks, and she wants her sister to know, but as she opens her mouth, a rumble from the trail ricochets down the coulee. She can make out the dancing headlights that have veered off the trail. A powder-blue Chevy pulls up beside their truck. Egg squints. The bright beams flash off and Kathy is already at the door, leaning into the open window. Egg would know that car anywhere.

"Stacey!" she calls out. She sees a pale arm wave from the window.

Egg doesn't know why her Mama hates Stacey Norman so much. Stacey's family is white and respectable. They grow yellow fields of canola by the flat plains and they have rose bushes instead of a vegetable garden. They go to church every Sunday but Mama calls them Episcopalians. Egg thinks that Mama doesn't trust any words that have so many vowels.

Kathy is always softer with Stacey around, as if the world lights up for her. Like Egg's honeybee lamp that makes the light go gold. When Kathy opens the door for Stacey, Egg realizes that Stacey makes her sister into a gentleman. Stacey Norman is a Damsel Fair.

When Stacey steps out of her car, it is as if she has stepped out of a magazine. Her clothes, all the way from Eighth Avenue Eaton's, have a glamour that seems out of place in Bittercreek.

Stacey's hair catches the firelight, like summer canola at dusk. As they approach, Egg hears Kathy mutter "detention," "rat Crawley," and Stacey's sympathetic reply.

Stacey's hand lights on Kathy's shoulder but she comes to Egg. She bends down to Egg's height and brushes back Egg's tumbled hair from her forehead.

"Oh, Egg. I heard what happened today. Are you all right?"

Egg shrugs.

"Well, maybe this will make the day better." Stacey places a stick of rock candy in Egg's hands.

"Wow! Thanks!"

Stacey always brings Egg rock candy after she visits her cousins in Niagara Falls. Niagara Falls is a Wonder of the World and rock candy is the best candy ever. Egg tears off the clear wrapping. It is a pink stick with a white centre—it has letters that go through the middle so it's like eating the alphabet. A sweet, crunchy alphabet that makes her mouth water.

Kathy and Stacey walk around the firepit. Their fingers entwine, fleetingly, such a hesitant touch that Egg pays it no mind. They are friends, Egg thinks, best friends. If only she could have a friend like that, how wonderful it would be. She snaps off a chunk of candy with a satisfying crack. They did not have rock candy in the Secret Annex. Anne Frank was so lonely; all she had was her diary. She was surrounded by her family, yet so alone. Egg wraps up her stick for later. If Anne were here, Egg would share it with her. Kathy has read to her of Anne's escape by railway. Kathy has told her that even the smallest can win. If you believe enough, you can do anything.

Darkness fills the coulee, this valley, like a river. On the upper slope, a pale glow touches the crest, like the very edge of frost.

Egg feels her goosebumps against sudden chill. Dusk dances on the horizon as the stars, awakening, blink open against the dark blue canvas of the night.

. . .

Egg sits in her bed, under the blankets, playing a game of Tent. Tent is like Maxwell Smart's Cone of Silence. But Tent can go anywhere. Tent is invisible.

Evel Knievel is back from his journey to the crawl space. Flashlight is with him. Sometimes Flashlight is the death-ray villain. In a story you have to have a villain, or some kind of fight. Egg pushes back the blanket. Sometimes Tent can get stuffy.

Egg thinks of the atmosphere, because if you are on another planet, you have a different atmosphere. She imagines herself somewhere else, someone else. But if she were someone else would she still be Egg?

If she could swim in the oceans like the big blue whale, would she still be herself? And what happens when you dream? In her dream the stairs go down but she tumbles up and the tornado comes and she's not afraid at all in this world that feels so real. When you sleep you have another life. Or is each dreaming a life of its own? Dreams are like kaleidoscopes—one twist and it's all different. Life can be like that too. One twist and it's all different.

No one talks about Albert. When Old Man Granger died, the whole town came out for his funeral. He was a man so mean he'd knock the shortening out of a biscuit, knock it two provinces across. Hornet mean. Buzzard mean. Even Mrs. Biddle, who has no teeth and could hardly walk, came to his funeral, and she came all the way from South Corner. Evangeline had missed her own father's funeral because she had gotten sick and was in the hospital. Egg forgot about that. There had been too many things to deal with. It was around the same time as Albert's accident at the railway trestle.

No one came to Albert's funeral. Well, Jack Henry and Dolores Henderson did, but where were all of Albert's friends?

Egg knows that when you're dead, your body goes into the ground and your soul goes into Heaven. But first there is Judgment. Reverend Samuels is big on Judgment. Kathy says that the Bible is begats and beholds and all about slave management. Egg thinks about Albert, and Heaven and the Ten Commandments. Sometimes she sees Kathy looking around the schoolyard and she knows that Kathy is searching for him, like she can't quite believe he is gone. Kathy never looks into his room and she never says his name. Egg thinks it must be like looking for your shadow and it's not there anymore. Albert was Kathy's big brother first, with barely a year between them. It was always Albert and Kathy, Kathy and Albert, the balance of opposites that kept the family's orbit tight. Egg wonders if a part of Kathy is mad at Albert but that doesn't make sense. It's not his fault he is dead. Albert was the boy, he was the important one, he was everything. Egg misses him but mostly she can't make sense of it all. How can dead be forever? She forgets sometimes and has to remind herself that dead is a hole in the ground. Dead is Mama raising Jesus in a baptism of whiskey and Papa in the ostrich barn and he won't come out.

Olly olly oxen free. Egg coughs. She holds a twist in her gut, a sudden, stabbing ache. She misses him. She squats, her knees against her chest. If she is still enough she can hold everything together.

Albert is over. Albert is done. Everything so bad since the railway trestle accident. Egg sits up as she blinks back her tears. Maybe it's not about being Japanese at all. Maybe it's about Albert, maybe that's when everything went wrong.

She pulls Tent over her and feels the air close and clinging. She sits in the comforting dark and tries to imagine herself different. Miss Granger says there is no limit to the imagination. Egg opens her eyes and she is still the same.

It is hard to make the imagination stick.

. . .

Mama is Not-Mama without Albert.

Yes. She loved him the best.

. . .

Jack-o'-lanterns, dancing skeletons, black cats, and witches — the school hallways are a nightmarish panorama of stark blacks and garish oranges. The Halloween Bash is in full swing with the requisite bedsheets and broomsticks, the corridors chock-o-block with cowboys and princesses as an echoey "Monster Mash" groans through the PA system.

Tonight, Egg can wear the Casper the Friendly Ghost mask (there are several Caspers roaming the halls — twenty-five cents at Gustafsson's General Store). Her old bedsheet, with a slit for her head, falls in a perfectly ghostly fashion. It is comforting behind the plastic mask, even if the nose holes are too small and her breath sounds like she has run the track seven times. With the cut-out eyes, the world seems close and contained. Kathy has dropped her off at the library entrance before joining the older years in the gym dance so Egg blends with the smaller ghouls, pirates, and hobos as they make their way to the doors of the library that swing open to the dark maw of the Haunted House.

When Albert was alive, the whole family would drive to their different neighbours for treats: Mama would chat with Dolores Henderson on the south border of the property, Papa and Jack Henry would have a beer on the west. Then Kathy would trek over to Stacey's and Albert would drop into town and they would all end up at the school for the Bash. But that is all over now. Tonight Mama is chasing phantoms with a bottle and Papa watches Griszelda, who is off her feed. Egg, in the Haunted House, steps under the cotton batten cobwebs strung over the aisles. A string of patio lanterns, decorated with shrieking black cats, their backs arched in cardboard terror, light the way. At the long table Egg thrusts her hands into bowls of cold boiled spaghetti and peeled grapes — innards and eyeballs. Barry Greenwood, with ketchup blood and plastic fangs, shoves her aside in his rush to get at the jello mould — "Look, I'm eating brains!" Egg's gaze travels over to the counter but Miss Granger is not there. Miss Chapman leans against the back shelves, her arms crossed. She is in her perfectly normal everyday clothes with her red lipstick and polished fingernails, yet she seems the spookiest of them all.

Egg scans the room. The witch's cauldron (on a fire made from strips of red and pink tissue paper) sits by the Halloween book display of *The Legend of Sleepy Hollow*, *Dracula*, and *Algebra for Everyone*. Bobbing for apples she will do without because she thinks of all the spit. Halloween is an odd thing, when villains become heroes and monsters roam the earth. Free candy is the best, even though Vice Principal Geary lurches down the hallway in a big wig and a polka-dot pantsuit as he doles out fistfuls of candies from his plastic pumpkin bin. His red nose is not a part of the costume.

Martin Fisken waves his wooden sword at Jimmy Simpson's head as he climbs onto a chair by the centre table. His skull-and-crossbones eye patch looks fancy; his luxurious vest is all city, a purple velveteen that sparkles with silver buttons.

Egg darts towards Upper Volta and the book cart. Even ghosts need to disappear sometimes. As she slips into the aisle, the stack of games by the witch's cauldron catches her eye. She stares. The box with two hands on a planchette against a background of stars—it is a Ouiji board. Before she even knows it she is at the cauldron, tucking the box under her bedsheet and darting behind the book cart. There, she has done it. Now she is a ghost and a thief.

. . .

In the darkness of the crawl space, Egg sits, as still as she can be. Below her, her father sleeps, restless in his cot, his snores filling the barn above the stamping and shuffling of the ostriches. Silently, she closes the shutter of the window. From beneath her ghost sheet, she pulls out the Ouiji box and unfolds the board. She lays it by the wooden crate, in front of her pile of precious *TV Guides*. The draft from the window brushes over her arms. Egg shivers. Carefully she places the planchette below the ornate letters of the alphabet, the gothic swirls and sharp angles, between the Hello and Goodbye. It's just a game, she tells herself, but her belly tickles and her throat is dry. Before she lights the candle with the matches from Mama's drawer, her eyes scan the space: her crate, the blanket, Evel Knievel watching from the ledge. Egg knows to conjure spirits there must be something more.

She scoots to the corner, to the ladder. The rungs lead down into a darkness that seems without end; even the candlelight cannot penetrate here. Egg steps into the shadow, moving by touch alone. It feels as if she is over a vast abyss, like the underwater divers in her *Young Reader's Guide to Science*. Her hands grasp the ladder as her foot slips, uncertain of the next step. Her toe points, a kick to find the next rung. Step. Step. She almost stumbles at the bottom of the ladder but her feet land on the solid dirt floor. Papa's snore, deep and even, fills the barn, above the gentle cooing of the chicks.

She reaches out to the shadows. She knows that Albert's boxes are right here but she thinks of all the things in the unknown dark.

A low chirp trills from the hatchling pen.

The chicks sit, bundled in the corner of the pen, a mass of fuzz. Only one has ventured from the clutch, its head rising, tilted, like a question mark.

"Esmeralda, go to sleep," Egg hisses. She looks hurriedly behind her. No ghosties, she thinks with relief.

Her father's wood stove casts a faint, cheerless glow. He does not stir beneath the clump of blankets coiled around his body. Cautiously, Egg opens a cardboard box and peers inside. Papa has kept everything, the trophies, the ribbons, the baby boots, and the baseball jersey, lucky number nine. No, not this box. She spies the suitcase. The squeak of the hinges makes her heart stop.

Esmeralda peeps.

"Shhh."

Inside the suitcase, she can make out Albert's plastic Roman soldiers, yellow and blue, his golden tie, the one for town. She feels the cool, stippled surface of his coin collection and his beloved Tetsuwan Atom key chain, the one all the way from Japan.

Egg remembers a dirt road, and a path that curved into green pine, leading to a meadow. Papa, Mama, Albert, and Kathy, they were all on a rare family vacation to the interior of British Columbia, in the heart of the Rockies. Egg loved the mountains, now so close, how she could see the bands of rock ripple and fold, the groves of fruit trees and the crisp, cold lakes that mirrored the sky. At a certain bend in the road they stopped to gather fiddleheads. Ostrich heads, Albert called them.

Papa, as he closed the door to the truck, had asked, "Is it here?"

They stumbled into a meadow, to a clump of shacks that were making their way back to forest. Ghost town. Small trees jutted through the boards of what was once a verandah, their branches clawing through the sagging roof. A rusted iron hand pump sat between the grey wooden cabins. Egg stared in wonder. Who lived here, once upon a time? Where did they go? She gazed at the darkened windows, at the rotting porch sprouting bushes, a rocking chair gone to mushrooms.

It seemed sad, this lonesome place. It was someone's home, abandoned and forgotten. Here, a door frame that held how many goodbyes. The canopy of the trees hushed in the gloom.

A deer bounded out of the thicket, darting, with a high kick, into the green woodlands.

A chattering burst of bird calls, then a sudden fall of silence.

Egg turned. Her Mama in a door frame.

"Egg!" Albert called.

In the meadow, Albert had found a rise and took Egg to the pitcher's mound. In this mountain hollow, with a stick for his bat, and an old bird's nest for his ball, he gave Egg pointers on the perfect pitch, the wind up, the hinge, the last-minute release.

"Make every pitch count," he said. "Make it like you're in the last inning, two strikes, three down, and the bases are loaded."

She watched him, his elegant toss, how he took the ball, forwards, then back, his Tetsuwan swinging from his belt loop. He moved so quickly, with such fluid grace, his pitcher's spin, like a pirouette.

Yes.

In the darkness of the barn, Egg holds Tetsuwan in her hand. The ostriches coo in their pens.

This is perfect.

Silently, she makes her way back up the ladder and sits in front of the Ouiji board with her offering.

She takes a deep breath, gazing at the wavering flame and the shadow dance. As she places her fingertips on the planchette, she whispers, "Albert."

The wind slithers through the gaps in the rooftop as the long beams creak and groan. Below her, the ostriches scrape and stamp, their wings twirling and blustery, with a flurry of chirps from the hatchlings.

Egg takes a shallow breath. "How do I make things right?"

An eerie calm washes over the barn. The hairs on her arms stand on end as her back stiffens. The planchette trembles. Egg's breath catches as she watches the shadows dart across the ceiling. The wind sounds a low moan across the roof before the shutters blast open, flooding the loft with a piercing cold. Egg shrieks, her knees slam the Ouiji board, knocking over the candle. The fluttering pages of the *TV Guide* feel the lick of flame and erupt in a burst of light. Egg stamps the fire—out out out—and the embers float harmlessly to ashes.

Out.

Egg holds her breath but her father does not wake. He turns with a groan on the cot, the ancient springs squeaking their protest as he shifts his weight and pulls his blanket over his head.

Egg climbs out the window, slides down the roof of the side shed, almost tumbling down the ladder. Across the gravel, to the house, up the stairs, into her warm bed, she tucks under her covers without even taking off her shoes.

Her heart thunders, she is panting so loudly. She has dabbled in the Occult, sent a message into the spirit world. She wonders, what would Mrs. MacDonnell say?

She asked. And Albert answered with fire.

November

The last light of day slips away from the barren fields. The downfall wind that rolls east of the Rockies bristles and snaps, roaring unimpeded across the foothills. The seasons can change in one hour, a lazy drizzle that lashes into flurries. Early winter storm. Egg, with her chin on the window pane, watches the snow whip and whirl. She blows against the fogging glass. Her breath, captured by the pane, whitens and freezes. She looks to the barn, the silver outline of frost, a pencil-thin sheen that glistens against the dark. As she leans forward, she feels the magnifying glass in her back pocket.

She's a detective now, even if Kathy won't let her watch *Columbo*. She is looking for clues. Ever since the Ouiji board on Halloween, she knows that Albert is helping her, he is showing her the way from Heaven.

She slides down the hall in her slippery socks and places her ear on Mama's door. Mama's breathing is deep and even. She is asleep and Kathy is out with the truck, no doubt with Stacey, so the coast is clear. Egg skips down to the kitchen and pulls out the magnifying glass and turns to the cellar.

The tall, grey cellar door, scarred and warped with many seasons, stands beside the pantry. A long rough gouge scores the wood across the bottom length. A black stain mars the upper corner. Egg can feel the icy draft rushing through the gap over the threshold, the eerie whistle that it makes. It breathes, she thinks, quelling the twist in her stomach. She grasps the knob, feels the shock of cold metal against her palm, and pushes the door open. A wave of frigid air washes over her. In the darkness of the stairwell, she gropes for the cord—*click*—the bald electric blub flickers on.

She raises the magnifying glass with a flourish. "Begone all monsters!" she wants to shout but it only comes out in a squeak.

Nothing.

A centipede scurries across the wall and Egg almost screams. It's all those legs. It scares her so much that she even pees a little.

Cautiously she makes her way down, hand on the dusty, wooden banister. With every step the stairway seems to lengthen. Every creak is an announcement that she is here, an intruder in this sunken realm of darkness, of silent creeping things. Her skin crawls against the damp, the seeping, insinuating chill. She stumbles and throws her hand against the wall—feels the crumbling red granules of the brick—and she rubs her palm against her shirt to get rid of that tacky, clinging grit. There is a peculiar smell of root cellars and rough woven sacks, of musty dark corners and things best left forgotten.

A crate of Mama's whiskey sits by the bottom of the stairs between a bag of rotting onions and a box of sprouting potatoes. Strange tools clutter the space—a sickle, a long saw, a scythe,

the rusting wheels of a broken baler. In the far corner of the basement, there is what looks like a table, covered with a ragged sheet.

She need only take a few steps and the table will be within her reach. Stories of mummies with their brains picked out through their noses and the Curse of King Tut's Tomb run through her head. Then she thinks of Marie Curie from her *Young Reader's Guide to Science.* Marie Curie discovered polonium and radium and the theory of radioactivity. She won two Noble Prizes but she paid the ultimate price. Egg thinks of the bravery of Marie Curie, so she reaches out her hand and steps forward.

She grabs the sheet. With one tug, it falls to the floor.

In front of her, there is a figure-eight rail with a roundabout and tunnel, even a country station stop. The forest is caught by a loop of track. Tiny figures stand on the platform, motionless, frozen in time. This is Albert's train set, Egg realizes, but he will never come for it now. It strikes her as sad, these patient figures, this abandoned track. As she runs her finger along the line of rail, she thinks of Albert's train by the railway trestle. Character is destiny. But Albert's train was an accident. Can destiny be an accident?

She thinks of Anne and her rescue. Kathy read it to her, of Anne in the last freight car, of the train hitch that came undone. Egg can almost imagine it, the thin black lines of the tracks against the white snow, the crystalline frost that had broken the link.

Ta-da! There are miracles after all.

Egg picks up a girl in a red dress, no bigger than her thumbnail, and places it in her palm, clenching it in her fist. She knows that Anne's escape was miraculous but so many got left behind. What happened to them? Kathy has told her that the Nazis "came to power" (how did they come to power?) and they persecuted the Jews, but then the war was won and it was happily ever after. Egg knows that bad things happen but how did something go so wrong—not just one wrong but a whole bunch of wrongs? What did all the good people do? Anne, all the way up in Amsterdam, had to go into hiding.

Egg plucks the toy station master from the platform and slips him into the freight car.

"What are you doing down here?"

Egg jumps.

Kathy stands at the foot of the stairs. Her glare could set the room on fire. "Where did you find this?"

Egg blinks. It was here all the time, she wants to say, but is that what Kathy is asking?

In this light, Kathy seems all edges. The naked electric bulb cuts shadows darkly and casts deep hollows under her eyes.

"It was Albert's, wasn't it?" Egg balances the freight car in one hand, with the steam engine in the other.

Kathy's mouth opens but she does not say a word.

Egg stuffs a small figure into the cargo car but Kathy snatches it from her. "What are you doing?" Kathy demands. She stares at the small toy in her hand and, just as suddenly, throws it back to Egg.

"There were so many people on the train with no food or water. I just wanted to see how many could fit in." Egg holds out the boxcar. "It looks like Anne's train."

Kathy stares at her sister, the figures, the train. Suddenly, Egg can see her shrinking, not like her big sister at all. Egg feels a plummet, like being thrown into the deep end of the pool, the sounds all crashing, close and yet so far, a strange and undefinable terror of all the things that she will never understand.

Kathy blurts, "Do the kids at school tell you, you stink like an ostrich?"

"I've been ostrichized." Egg holds up a small figure. "You see, they had to wear yellow stars."

Kathy steps back. Her voice is dry, as it splinters. "Go to bed, Egg."

Egg tries to understand. "Are you mad because it's Albert's?"

"Go to bed, Goddamnit!"

Egg runs up the stairs. It's not fair. Just because Kathy is big-sister-bossy-the-cow does not mean she is right. Why is she so angry anyway?

Albert knows. He has left the clues. Why else the train track and this girl in the lonely dark?

Egg places the small figure of the girl in the red dress on her bedside table, in the golden light of her honeybee lamp. This one, she will be safe in the annex. This one, so small and fragile, just like Anne Frank.

. . .

In the library Egg sits below Ancient History with the *Oxford* on her lap. Today is an *S* day: silly, sappy, sacrosanct. Everyone needs an *S* day. Kathy has been having a whole slew of *S* days; her smile never leaves her face. Egg likes the word *spilth*. *Splosh* and *splutter* are also her favourites, even if you can only have one favourite. *S* makes the most sense in the alphabet. It is most like itself, that's why snakes begin with the letter *S*, why small *s* and capital *S* stay the same. Rivers meander into *s*'s and eternity is two *s*'s kissing. Egg calls it kissing even though they are lying down.

The opposite of *s* is *o* and that is why SOS is like that. When you need help. *O* you fall into. *O* is a surprise. *O* and zero equal each other.

X is another story altogether.

Martin Fisken got into a fight with Ronald Grimchuk. Martin got hurt real bad. Egg gave him a candy from her lunch but he only stepped on it and kicked it away. Bullies are like that. Sometimes mad is all they got. Martin boasted that his name was called on *The Buck Shot Show* because he wrote in for his birthday. Only townies can see *The Buck Shot Show* during lunchtime. Egg doesn't know what the big deal is anyway.

This was after Martin showed his pen-is to the girls in the schoolyard. Egg called it a pen-is but he said it was called a pee-nis because pee comes out of it. Egg thinks that is gross, like swishing jello through your teeth, spitting it out, then drinking it. She knows that S - E - X is two people mashing up against each other and making babies. Egg thinks that something is wrong with Martin's pen-is. It's all wrinkly and ugly.

S - E - X is called Original Sin but Egg doesn't understand why it is a sin to make babies.

She thinks that if there are rules, people should tell you them, else you just get into trouble and it's really not your fault. How are you supposed to not talk about something if they don't tell you what to not talk about? Then Mrs. MacDonnell just starts turning red and it's out the door for you.

. . .

Time crawls in Mrs. Syms's afternoon class. It is after lunch and Egg's head feels heavy. Insects with exoskeletons, with the bones on the outside. Egg wonders how you can make insects boring.

There is a knock on the door and thirty-two heads look up.

A blond puffball that is Mrs. Jonas's head pops into the classroom. Behind her trails a shadow. At the blackboard, Mrs. Syms stiffens, the chalk snaps in her fingers, and she goes to the door.

The class is strangely silent, strangely still.

When Mrs. Syms turns, she holds a girl in front of her.

But oh, what a girl! She is so much bigger and older and from another country. Her skin is dark brown, like earth after rain, and she is wrapped up in orange and gold. The other girls in the class smirk and whisper—jealous, Egg thinks. But this one, she seems so soft, so warm that Egg wants to curl up beside her.

"Now. We have a guest. A late. Addition." Mrs. Syms does not sound pleased. Mrs. Syms sounds as if she is swallowing a three-foot pickerel. "Tell them your name, child. Quickly, the class is waiting."

The girl does not say a word.

Mrs. Syms huffs and puffs. "It's Kuldeep." Egg can see Mrs. Syms's teeth when she says this.

The pickerel wriggles in Mrs. Syms's gullet and her talons are out as she pushes Kuldeep to the back of the class. The corner desk is pulled from the back corner, dragged beside Egg. Egg sits up, back straight, biting down on her lip. She could almost squeal with delight.

As Mrs. Syms turns away, Egg steals a glance at Kuldeep. Kuldeep's hands are folded over a copy of *Charlotte's Web* and two new notebooks. Egg scans Kuldeep's desk; there is no pencil case. Egg places her best HB yellow pencil (no bite marks) on the edge of Kuldeep's desk and slides it carefully towards Kuldeep's hands.

Kuldeep's eyes widen, her head dipping into the slightest bow. Egg's stomach does cartwheels.

At recess Egg shows Kuldeep the girl's washroom, the water fountain, the glass doors to the library. As Egg chatters about the jungle gym, the school bus, and the lunchroom, the sound bounces off the cavernous walls of the hallway. She launches into how bats use echolocation in the dark, how the *Young Reader's Guide to Science* explains this. Kuldeep takes in the yard, the green, the long grey line of withering maples, all with her great brown eyes. She looks so lost and alone that Egg wants to take her hand and tell her everything will be okay. But Egg's words tumble faster and faster, about the bully gang and never to eat the Wednesday lunch special and how the *Mutual of Omaha* shows you that camouflage is the best defence. Egg tells her about the library and Anne Frank and the running speed of ostriches. Gravity is a force of nature and the speed of light is the fastest ever.

As Egg catches her breath, Martin and Chuckie run in front of them in their game of Cowboys and Indians. Bang bang and you're dead, and the sprawling hit and stagger that drags out across the playground. But the cowboys always get up again. Cowboys never lose because they are the good guys.

There is a chill in Egg's stomach. Kuldeep is an Indian and what does she make of this game? Bang bang and Egg can see that Kuldeep is sad. It's just a game, she wants to say, but something is wrong and she doesn't have the words. Charlotte saved Wilbur with letters spun from a spider's web, so surely Egg could so the same. Egg reaches out for Kuldeep's hand. Her fingers hesitate. They touch and the shock of Kuldeep's flesh rushes to Egg's core. Kuldeep's eyes are the warmest brown but Egg feels that Kuldeep does not fit into this washed-out, wind-scored desert. The light is harsh, the air unkind.

A ball hurls towards Kuldeep and without a thought, Egg steps out and smacks it away. Amazed, she stares at her hand, feels the sting against her palm, savours it. She blinks. Character is destiny.

Yes, she can change. She can be the strong one.

. . .

That night, Egg climbs into the barn loft and pulls her notebook from beneath the safety of her shirt. Egg thinks about the scientific method from her *Young Reader's Guide to Science*. The scientific method always begins with a question. Stories are like that, they are a big "what if?" Stories and science make sense of the world. That is why the story of Galileo makes more sense to her than the science of Galileo. The story makes him alive. Like Claudia Kincaid running away to the Metropolitan Museum of Art in the *Mixed-Up Files of Mrs. Basil E. Frankweiler.* But Anne Frank is different. She is real. Anne Frank tells you how the world is so you know that you're not the only one who is lonely or misunderstood. She tells you hang in there because the railway train will come to the rescue. There is a light at the end of the tunnel.

Egg writes down:

Kuldeep.
Did she come from a war?
Can she talk at all?
What does she like?

How can I make her smile?

Egg puts down her pencil and rubs her head. She knows what she needs. She needs to be Popular. If she were Popular, she wouldn't have to worry about Martin. If she were Popular, she would be able to help Kuldeep. If she were Popular, Mama and Papa would not miss Albert so much and they would not be so sad.

Below her, the ostriches scratch and flare as they kick at the grill and hiss at the bars. The ostriches, with their black plume and white edge feathers. They come all the way from Africa, southern "blacks" her father calls them. She knows about the Indian reservations; Vice Principal Geary said they have their own schools called Residentials. Egg wonders why there aren't any Indians in Bittercreek now. She has read about apart-hate, even though Kathy has tried to hide *The Globe and Mail* from her. Kathy picks up her stack of newspapers every week from Gustafsson's store. She says that Current Events are not kid's stuff, yet Kathy has read the *Globe* for as long as Egg can remember. Egg knows that Kathy tries to shield her from the world but the world is all around her.

Egg knows that the world has categories, an order, an agenda. For everything there is a time and there is a place, in Heaven and on Earth, a plan for the weak and the mighty, from the greatest, most brightest star to the smallest, most tiniest atom. The world holds the big blue whale and the bumblebee bat. That means somewhere, in the middle, there must be a place for her.

. . .

Egg cradles the bundle on her lap as the school bus rolls over the ruts and rises of the gravel road. She is extra careful today, extra small. It is the end-of-the-week Show and Tell and she wants so much for Kuldeep to like her surprise.

As she walks to her desk she gives Kuldeep a big smile and it doesn't matter that Martin almost trips her. First is spelling and then mathematics. Egg squirms in her seat. This day is taking forever but the bundle is safe under her desk. Last week Mrs. Syms had said no more toys after Mary Margaret McDougall brought in her Baby Alive, Newborn Baby Tenderlove, and a Wake Up Thumbelina. Barry Greenwood shattered his Klackers, cutting his chin on the very first try, and was sent to the nurse's office. At the jungle gym, Martin and Chuckie snapped little Jimmy Simpson's Stretch Armstrong in two in a tug of war at recess, so it was a disaster all around. But this week Egg knows that her Show and Tell is different. Her Show and Tell is Science.

In the last period, Mrs. Syms calls out Egg's name and Egg takes the long walk to the front of the class with a bundle in her arms. As she turns to face her classmates, her stomach jumps up in her throat. There is a spasm in her belly and she feels like she has to pee. Mrs. Syms stifles a yawn as she straightens her desk, her ruler in hand, poised and ready for any infraction. Egg takes a deep breath and uncovers the newspaper wrapping.

The egg is almost as large as Egg's head, a cream-coloured

orb that dwarfs her hand. At the base, a small segment has cracked away to a jagged edge. Here, the thickness of the shell can be seen. Monstrously huge and vaguely reptilian, she holds it before her. The class, in spite of itself, leans forward and Mrs. Syms actually puts down her ruler.

Egg begins by telling her classmates that ostriches have a claw and a kick that could break the jaw of a lion. Ostriches vomit in their water trough and the smell would make your nose hairs fall out.

"Ewwww," the class shrieks.

Ostriches can run up to forty miles an hour and their knees bend the opposite way. They are over eight feet tall and have two different kinds of eyelids. Egg's voice shakes only a little as she tells the class that the ostrich egg is the biggest in all the world — almost five pounds, like twenty-four chicken eggs. Ostriches can live for up to seventy years and they eat stones to grind up the food in their stomachs. Sometimes they stargaze, their necks bent backwards. They twirl but no one knows why.

At the end Egg leans forward and caps it all off with, "When they're chicks, they have to eat poop!" as her classmates explode into giggles.

She gives everyone a piece of the white tendril fluffs but to Kuldeep she hands a whole back tail plume. "For you," Egg chirps. Kuldeep seems not to have understood a word but her eyes sparkle. There is the smallest nod. And then a miracle: a smile.

· · ·

Egg jumps off the last steps of the school bus, her arms out, an airplane. She's Popular, she's Popular! The world has changed in some small way. Even the sky looks different; the clouds tumble, and have flyaway wisps—like feathers, Egg thinks, like wings. The wind tousles her hair, the air is brisk against her cheeks. She stands straight. Why, she has even grown taller, she can feel it!

She runs down the line of the pens, her arms stretched out.

"Wooh woooh wooooooh" she cries.

She stops in her tracks. She wants something special for Monday and she knows just the thing.

Her father rakes the outside pens. Egg knows that he will take at least ten minutes by the grill. She sneaks into the barn through the gate, past the barred enclosures, to Albert's boxes. She knows where the suitcase is, the one with the golden tie. His lucky one. The one he used to wear to town.

Black, with gold swirls. Like a midnight sky with shooting stars.

Loop over loop, she tries it. She remembers Albert's slicked-back hair, the scent of his pomade. Funny, she never asked who he was spiffing up for. His laughter, so disarming, was good enough for her.

She's almost got it right, she wants Kuldeep to see her with swirling gold, a starry night. Slip, up near the collar and through the knot—she tugs and the loop unravels, slipping through her fingers to the floor.

Damn. She stoops to pick up the coil but a skinny neck, covered in the softest down, pokes through the adjacent bars. The beak plucks at the fabric and begins to swallow the end.

"Esmeralda!" Egg exclaims. She grabs the loop and pulls in this tug of war with an ostrich gullet.

"Let. It. Go!" Egg yanks hard and the wet end splats against her forehead. She holds up starry night, a slippery, slimy mess and sniffs.

She wrinkles her nose. There is no way that she can wear that to school.

Damn. Damn. Damn. Egg glares at Esmeralda and huffs, "At least you didn't swallow it."

Esmeralda twirls, as if she doesn't know what all the fuss is about.

The chick has grown so quickly, the quirky head, as big as Egg's fist, bobs on the fuzzy neck. Esmeralda was only eight inches when she was hatched, barely one-and-a-half pounds but she has grown two feet since then. Even so she is still the smallest one. Esmeralda's head pops up, like a prairie dog from its hole. Her head jerks left, then right. Egg thinks of a submarine's periscope and she giggles. Esmeralda is almost as tall as Egg's shoulder.

Almost. Esmeralda fluffs her wings but Egg knows that if she wet down her feathers, Esmeralda would be as thin as a stick. There is a scratch on Esmeralda's left foot, just on top of her big toe. Egg feels a ripple of fear rush up her spine. Old Yeller dies. So does the Yearling. Egg has seen it all on *The Wonderful World of Disney*. Lemmings that rush the cliff and the awful fate of those stuck in the Tar Pits. Even Wilbur almost becomes Christmas dinner. All but for Charlotte.

Egg furrows her brow, trying to remember Charlotte's words. "Some Pig," the spider had written. But was Wilbur really some extraordinary pig or was he really just lucky? The real hero, the one in the shadows, the one who toils and triumphs, is Charlotte the spider. Egg consoles herself that at least Charlotte, with her pluck and intelligence, at least she shines when the truth is revealed, when Charlotte and Wilbur go to Las Vegas.

Kathy had been especially pleased after reading *Charlotte's Web* to Egg. They even celebrated with Jiffy Pop.

Egg strokes the down on Esmeralda's head, the fine hairs that ridge her brows. She feels the pulse of life through her fingertips, that strange soft-hard feeling of bone beneath the skin. A shot of fear runs through her. What if she can't protect Kuldeep? What if she is not strong enough? Egg thinks of her father in the ostrich barn as he rakes the outside pen. *Shhh shhhh shhhh*, the stroke of the tines against the grass. Her chest feels heavy as she wonders. What if she fails? What would that mean?

Esmeralda bunts her head against Egg's hand. She looks down into the ostrich chick's brown eyes. Egg thinks that eyes are miracles. Do ostriches have souls? Will ostriches go to Heaven? Papa says animals have instincts, that there is no choice in the matter. Human beings have choices but didn't Eve sin for us all?

Egg strokes Esmeralda's head. There must be a Heaven for ostriches; there must be some kind of point to it all. She knows that fair is fair but the Bible is not always fair. It troubles Egg, like the glimpse of a rat's tail darting by the feed, or the rustling in the walls as the shadows draw long into the winter's night.

But Esmeralda, Egg thinks, Esmeralda. She has a name now. She can be saved.

. . .

On Saturday she decides. On Saturday she has a mission.

Chinook wind basks the day in warm breezes as an arch of low-lying clouds hover near the horizon. The brilliant sun shines overhead. Chinook wind takes the winter away, peels back the frost, as if to say winter take a holiday, your time will come but not today.

Egg likes to rhyme.

She rides her banana-seat bike out to where the flat plains drop, her tires *click click click* as the hockey cards snap against her spokes. Faster and faster, she thinks she is flying as she rolls down the slope of the drop. She tries to ride hands-free but the ground is too bumpy. Here, under the thousand shades of blue, that's where she feels everything is so small and so big at the same time. She pedals out to the lone erratic on the plain, a massive stone swept down by ancient glaciers in the last ice age. The abandoned rock sits on the edge of Jansson's field. She lifts herself up on the lip of the rock, the texture rough beneath her hands. She is climbing Everest, grunting as she shimmies up the central fissure, her hands grabbing the top as she pulls herself up and over.

"Wooh woooh wooooooh!"

From the top of the erratic, she can see the railway trestle in the distance, and to her left, the hoodoos with their top-caps, where the Badlands begin.

She slaps her hands together, knocking off the dirt. Her finger traces the vein in the speckled granite. Igneous, sedimentary, metamorphic. Even the rocks have a story.

She takes out Evel Knievel from the inside of her jacket. She can see her shadow as the sun scurries out from the cover of the clouds. As she pulls out the magnifying glass from her back pocket, she lays Evel on the flat rock. There, on the ancient erratic, she burns out Evel Knievel's eyes, focusing the beam of light. A wisp of smoke rises from the blackening plastic. There is always a sacrifice. Wages of Sin is Death. Someone always pays but it is not going to be her.

"Better safe than sorry," she says. For Esmeralda, for Kuldeep. Burn out the evil in her. Let the melting eyes absolve her. Egg, the not-good-enough as Albert, Egg, the useless one at home. Now that she is Popular, let it be enough. Egg prays. Let all the bad be over.

. . .

Egg bikes home, along the top of the ridge. Her hands are off the handle bars, her arms stretched wide. She doesn't see the rut on the ground. Her front wheel twists, and she keels forward, over the bars. Landing hard, she slides down the exposed sandy slope into a trough. She digs her heels in and stops at the very edge of the hole.

Whew, she thinks. That was close.

She stares at the hole. It is like a gap in the world itself, a darkness bordered by four roughly hewn wooden planks. The planks are unusually thick, thicker than the abandoned railway ties that occasionally line the trail. Gouges mark the wood, a blackened strip that a flame must have branded. Her fingers trace the score, the run of the grain as she cautiously peers into the hole.

Dark and deep.

She rocks back.

She looks behind her and finds a rock the size of her head. With two hands she holds it, then heaves it over the edge. Crash, plunk, thud, off the walls, against wood and stone. There seems to be no end to the descent.

A well, Egg thinks. A hole big enough to stuff all the ugly in the world.

As she looks over the edge of the pit, the walls of dirt and wooden beams weave, they tilt and slant, she feels a sudden vertigo.

She scrambles away on her hands and feet, away from that lulling deep. She dashes up the slope to her bike and grasps the coolness of the handle bars.

She cannot stop shaking.

She pulls up her bike and runs, jumps on her banana seat away from the well. She rides, pedalling furiously until she reaches the path.

At the rise in the trail, she puts her foot down, braking into a skid as the back wheel slides to a halt. She looks back.

All she can see is the flat field.

She blinks, the sweat stinging her eyes.

Her glance falls to a small protruding curve that lies in the dirt, half-buried near her foot. She digs at the curve, her fingers curl around the smooth surface and pull it from the dirt. It is a bone, a claw. It is the size of her hand. She looks to the field. A gift from the well, she thinks.

Later, as Kathy tucks her in, Egg dangles the tip of the claw bone off the tip of her finger. Egg thinks, sabretooth. Egg thinks, mammoth. The sheer enormity of the beast makes her wonder. Her stomach hurts so much that she squishes Nekoneko under her armpit.

Kathy frowns. "Shouldn't be playing with bones you dug up. Get lockjaw or something. I'm not even going to ask where you got that cut."

Egg touches her forehead but she doesn't feel the ache. She looks to the door. "Where's Mama?"

Kathy hesitates. "She's not feeling so good." She glances at the figure under the bedside lamp, the girl in the red coat and she frowns. "Did you eat anything?"

Egg leans over and points to her plate on the floor. A crust of bread with some flecks of hard corned beef.

"Are you eating under the bed again?" asks Kathy.

"I'm in hiding," Egg says.

Kathy glances at the cat puppet in Egg's armpit, squeezed like bagpipes. "Aren't you a little old for Nekoneko?"

"No, look." Egg opens the bottom of Neku. Inside, there is a chocolate bar. "For food," Egg explains, "for when they take us away."

"That'll never happen," Kathy says, with irritation. But she shifts. "It was wartime."

"They always say it's wartime."

Kathy pulls up the blanket with a snap, tight around Egg.

"Tell me about the dog," Egg says.

"What?"

"The spaceship you like. Spudnick."

"Sputnik."

"The one with the dog."

"Laika. She went up with Sputnik and she was the first living thing in space."

"Like an explorer."

"Yes."

"She got a medal and everything. She was a hero."

"Yea—"

"And then she had a parade when she got back. And the Russians made her into a cosmonaut."

"Good night, Egg."

Egg snuggles down but her eyes are open. She thinks of her bone from the field. "Kathy, do you think it's a human bone?"

Kathy snorts. "Not unless we grew claws in the last century."

"Maybe it's like Buffalo Jump, in the olden days, when they killed a lot of Indians."

"I'm turning off the light." Kathy stands and walks to the door.

Egg rises on her elbows. "If Jesus was a Jew, why did He let all those people die?"

Kathy is ready to slam the door but she catches herself. "I don't know. And they didn't all die. The Indians, I mean." The door clicks shut and then she is gone.

Egg thinks about the day. The well. She didn't tell Kathy about the well. She tries to think about looking over the edge into the unknown. She can't explain what she felt there. Maybe there is no word for it.

She tries to imagine herself falling. Would it be like Major Tom, a hundred thousand miles away? Major Tom floats in his tin can, across the universe. She thinks of the earth spinning in orbit, the sun in the galaxy of a billion stars. She would like to float, to fly.

She taps her feet together. "Cumulus nimbus," she whispers, because she likes the words.

. . .

There are perks to being Popular. Martin Fisken has not bothered her in days. He has taken up tormenting Jimmy Simpson in the playground. Egg has discovered that she actually does like sitting in the lunchroom, watching all the students as they mill about their tables. It is almost a week since her Show and Tell but Kuldeep has been away for most of it. Egg has taken extra notes so Kuldeep doesn't fall behind. She has drawn giraffes in the margins.

Kuldeep is in class today.

But today is gym class. Egg hates gym class.

An accordion wall splits the boys from the girls. In the girls' gym section, Mrs. MacCloskey is all barking commands and arms akimbo. She lines up her class two-by-two. Mrs. MacCloskey, who looks like a Scottish terrier, is all about drills and formations. She tells the class that they will be building character and co-operation. Egg hates two-by-two, the scramble for a partner, the flash of panic of not being picked. Two-by-two and time crawls, rejection after rejection, two-by-two and Glenda looks at you like you have the cooties, or that you really smell. But today is different. Today Egg is Popular. Janice James takes Egg's hand. It is just like the loaves and fishes. Egg doesn't have time to contemplate this miracle, as Janice tugs her from the line. Is seems so easy, a mere step out of the pariah zone.

Egg looks back and sees Kuldeep in the line, standing by herself. The others shuffle away from her, as if fearful of contagion. Egg sees Kuldeep's tears and grips Janice's hand. She wants to explain to Kuldeep that she needs to be Popular for the both of them but the look in Kuldeep's eyes does not waver. Egg knows that something is wrong, she feels it in the pit of her stomach, eating away at her but she can't let go of Janice's hand. She can't let go of Popular.

A small voice whispers in her ear: what's the use of having Kuldeep for a friend when she can't even speak English anyways?

The next day Kuldeep is not in class and her desk is pushed into the corner.

Egg feels a twist in her stomach as she raises her hand.

Mrs. Syms's eyebrows rise. "Yes?"

"Where is Kuldeep?"

Mrs. Syms's eyes narrow. She looks to the empty space where Kuldeep used to sit and her lips tighten into an adder's grin. "Oh, that girl. It turns out that Bittercreek is not the most suitable place for her family. Well, not all of us can have that pioneer spirit. Now let's turn to page thirty-four in *Call Us Canadians*, shall we?"

At recess Egg runs to the bushes by the jungle gym and squats behind the tangle of branches. If no one sees you, then you disappear. Egg closes her eyes. She tucks her knees up to her chest and twists her shoelaces with her fingers.

Kuldeep is gone and Egg has betrayed her. It isn't Albert at all. There is something in Egg that brings out the ugly, even if she is Popular.

There is a scream from the jungle gym.

Egg's eyes snap open at the sound. Little Jimmy Simpson struggles, on tiptoe, as Martin Fisken wraps his fingers around Jimmy's throat. Jimmy's eyes bulge, like the boy in the swimming safety film that everyone watches at the summer pool. A roar fills Egg's ears. She blinks and she is suddenly in front of Martin's face, her fists windmilling. Martin looks surprised. He lets go of Jimmy, who crumples at his feet. Jimmy scoots away sideways, like a crab, without a backwards glance.

Martin grins.

That's it. Egg wants to knock the freckles out of Martin Fisken's face, even if he is so much taller. She raises her fist and draws it back, like the pitcher's throw, a curveball in the last inning, three down, and the bases loaded. All her frustration is packed in that windup, all her confusion, all the hurt for Kuldeep. Take out all the bad and throw it into Martin Fisken's fox face. Her knuckles curl, her whole body hurls forward. That's when Vice Principal Geary's hand comes down out of the blue and grabs her wrist and it is off to the Principal's office for her.

. . .

That night, Egg sprawls in front of the television with her notebook in front of her. The television is off. No more television, not for a week. That's her punishment for being sent to the Principal's office even if it is Not Her Fault. Kathy was sympathetic, turning Egg's Not Her Fault into a Next Time Don't Get Caught. It's not fair, Egg complained, Martin pushes and Martin shoves but he never gets sent to the Principal's office.

My point exactly, Kathy said.

Mama said, God sees everything and He knows what happened. But still no television for a week.

Egg stares wistfully at the blank television screen. She writes in her notebook:

> If God knows everything, why doesn't He do anything about the bad?
> If He can't do anything, what's the point about being God?

The Dictionary says God is the Supreme Being, who is the creator and ruler of the universe.

But what does that mean?

"Egg?"

Egg looks up from her notebook. She squeezes her eyes to focus her vision. Kathy looks at her, concerned.

"What?" Egg asks.

"Your nose is sticking to that page." Kathy purses her lips. "Can you see all right?"

Egg wants to disappear.

After much peering and poking, Mama and Kathy drive Egg up to Calgary for an eye doctor's appointment, that strange contraption of revolving glass discs and a slice of light that flashes across the eyes. The grown-ups talk above her, all drones and clucks and heavy sighs, then Egg is hauled off to an eyeglass store (not eyes that are made out of glass) as chunks of glass and twisted wire are placed upon her nose. Mama and Kathy bicker and pout but Egg puts up with it all.

Because Egg has figured it all out.

This is logic. She's read about it in the *Young Reader's Guide to Science*, something the ancient Greeks used to do, like Doctor Spock in *Star Trek*. Doctor Spock is an alien from his home planet of Vulcan but he looks kind of Japanese too. Logic makes sense in the world. It's simple, really. Egg, sitting in the squeaky vinyl chair in the eyeglass shop, finally puts two and two together.

Divine Retribution. Her glasses are a form of Divine Punishment. Coming so soon after Kuldeep's departure, it is clearly a sign from above. Because things have a reason. So Reverend Samuels preaches. Every equal and opposite thing, even Newton says.

Egg blinks. The clarity of it blinds her but it is only the reflection of a mirror thrust in front of her face.

"Do you like this, sweetpea?" her mother inquires.

Egg nods at everything. She will have the patience of saints and angels. Things have a purpose, things have a place. She will bear the weight of the world, the burden of the ages, all because of God's great plan. For there must be a plan, there must be a God, there must be a final reckoning when the curtain goes up and the people kneel down and all the voices come together and cry, this is how I have suffered, this is how I have kept the faith, like in all the Sunday afternoon television programs but without all the velvet. The running of mascara like the blood of Jesus from his crown of thorns. There must be a God, a truth and atonement, the burning bush and the sacrificial lamb, there must be a place and a purpose, for if there isn't, then there is nothing. A nothing so terrible that Egg can only creep back from the edge.

The well. A nothing like the well.

If it is nothing, then there is no answer. If God is just a magician with fancy tricks, then everything is a lie. The world is a lie. A black hole of nothingness and no one can ever get out. All the goodness and light get sucked into it. No Moral of the Story.

Egg clasps her hands and prays. *I will be good. I will be good.* Thy kingdom come, thy will be done, on Earth as it is in Heaven.

Let there be a Heaven.

A Heaven to make sense of the world. A Heaven for Albert.

. . .

With her wire-rimmed glasses perched precariously on her nose, Egg steps off the school bus. Everything looks different. The sun glances, brilliant against the ice-coated bars of the jungle gym. The last remnants of the night's hoarfrost sparkle in the tiny fissures in the concrete. The world seems sharp, all edges.

Today, she is the four-eyed freak and everybody knows it.

Careful. Careful.

At lunchtime, Egg steps out to the schoolyard from the library doors. She sees Martin Fisken by the bleachers. He is screaming. His brother, Doug Fisken, surrounded by his gang, holds him up by his hair. Martin's legs are kicking frantically, fists flailing, his cheeks a bright and ruddy red.

His brother just laughs. Egg can see his teeth.

A sound catches in Egg's throat as she stares at Martin's tears. It's fair, though. Is it? Isn't it? Retributive justice. Egg looked it up in the Dictionary.

Douglas Fisken, star of the football team. Not a championship team, but this year, his senior year, he is the top dog in Bittercreek. He has his picture in the *Calgary Herald* and everything. Before, Doug was always in the shadow of Albert. Albert was smaller but smarter, and his baseball team went all the way to the finals.

Doug, who calls Raymond "sissyface" and "faggot."

Egg steps back through the library doors. A knot hardens in her chest. She would not wish Douglas Fisken on anyone.

She must be careful. She will not feel sorry for Martin. Not one bit.

She feels the heat in her cheeks as she closes the door.

. . .

Egg jumps off her bed. She knows that there are terrible things in the world, terrible things. She has chosen not to put all her eggs in one basket. Beneath her bed, there is a stash of Hereford

Canned Corned Beef and all the tin keys she has collected, rattling in a Callard's toffee tin. She hoards the pieces of last year's chocolate Easter Bunny that one-eared, one-eyed Nekoneko guards. Nekoneko Kitty has one eye that never sleeps.

Run, run, run as fast as you can, a part of her shouts, her mind a-tumble with all the king's horses and all the king's men. Anne Frank had to run.

Egg stares out her window. The clouds streak across the sky, as if clawed out of the blue by some fabulous, ferocious beast. She drops to the floor, rolling; she knows how to take a dive. Not for the first time, she wishes for wings, like in *D'Aulaires' Greek Myths*. If she could get on the *$10,000 Pyramid*, she'd be sure to take the prize. All of Bittercreek would be cheering for her and Dick Clark would shake her hand on *American Bandstand*. Anything could happen. Why, if you look at the news, England's full of bombings and planes fall out of the sky, even Skylab could destroy a city the size of Detroit, so they say.

She grabs her rubber ball and crashes it into her dinky cars.

Boom boom bomb.

Lego smash.

History is a once upon a time. The bad wars were a long time ago. History is about things getting better so the horrible things are worth it, just like Newton's equal and opposites. That is why you must grin and bear it, why there is a great and Heavenly plan. Egg knows that God demands sacrifices but at least Anne Frank is alive. If one good thing survives, then it is worth it. That one good thing she can hold onto.

She jumps on the bed again, and swings back her arm, like Albert taught her for the killer pitch. Albert's curve ball, the secret in the finger split. Egg remembers his photograph in *The*

Bittercreek Bulletin, as the Bittercreek Athlete of the Year, with Douglas Fisken sulking beside him.

Yes, Egg thinks. Now she knows where to go.

. . .

With the magnifying glass in her back pocket, Egg scoots down to the vertical drawers of the school library where the newspapers hang through the bars. *The Bittercreek Bulletin* is a four-page weekly that Mrs. Heap from Heap's Hardware churns out (weather, cattle, and canola) but bigger news usually goes to the *Calgary Herald*. The hanging sheets are too recent so Egg roots under the shelf for the stacks.

She finds the date:

Calgary Herald

May 26, 1974
Tragic Accident Claims Two in Crash
Two residents of the town of Bittercreek, Alberta, were killed when their vehicles collided with a Canadian Pacific train late Saturday evening. Another occupant of the colliding trucks was taken to hospital with non-life threatening injuries.

Thomas Earle Granger, 54, of Bittercreek, Alberta, and Albert Henry Murakami, also of Bittercreek, were both killed when their trucks were struck at the rail crossing by the Langhorn Trestle Bridge.

Police report that the trestle bridge has not been damaged. CP spokesman Ronald Greschuk says there are no injuries of the CP crew.

Mr. Greschuk says a full investigation into the cause of the crash is under way, although an initial review has determined that all the CP systems were functioning as intended.

Shock rippled throughout the small community as news of the deaths were announced. Thomas Granger was an upstanding resident of the Bittercreek community, son of Louis Granger who established the new Bittercreek United Church on Main.

Prominent resident Harold Fisken commented, "It's a very unfortunate event. Our thoughts and prayers are with the families."

Alcohol has been ruled out as a factor in this tragedy.

Egg gasps. Albert was not alone by the trestle bridge. Evangeline's father was also in the accident. Two trucks struck at the rail. How did that happen? Is this why no one came to Albert's funeral? Was the accident his fault?

Egg looks around her to see if the coast is clear. With one firm tug, she rips the article from the page and stuffs it into her pocket. Evidence, she thinks. But for what, she does not yet know.

. . .

In church, Reverend Samuels went over the Ten Commandments and Egg is pretty sure Thou Shalt Not Take the Lord's Name in Vain was up there. But she also heard Mr. Geary swear "Goddamnit" when he smashed his fingers. The whole school heard. It was on the PA system. And then there was a string of words that she can't even remember.

From the pulpit Reverend Samuels crows about how prayer is the answer. Beside Egg, in the last pew, Kathy folds her hands and whispers, "Dear God: about this war business. Not the greatest invention." And, "Famine. Your point is?" Egg is scared when Kathy says, "Earthquakes. Not the best way to rearrange the furniture."

Kathy is going to burn in Hell.

Egg knows it's bad to steal but Mrs. MacDonnell has a whole bowl of itty bitty plastic Jesuses in her drawer at Sunday school. Egg scoops them out when Mrs. MacDonnell is not looking. It's not that she's stealing. She's just borrowing them to save Kathy's soul. She'll put them in Kathy's lunch bag and under her pillow. Kathy can't find them all, Egg figures, so maybe one of them will stick. Kathy needs all the help she can get. And God is there to help, isn't He?

All her life, Egg has heard about the three-in-one God, the everything, all-you-can-eat God. God is Great. God is Good. Mrs. MacDonnell says you can see God in a beautiful flower. A flower's a flower. Egg thinks, shouldn't you see God in all flowers and not just the pretty ones? Mrs. MacDonnell says not all prayers get answered and that's just God's Way and then Egg wonders, what is the point? Does it mean there are some Commandments we can skip?

God is vengeance, God is love. Kathy says God has a multiple personality disorder. Egg is still looking that up in the dictionary.

As she gazes over the congregation, she can see that all of Bittercreek is here, even Mrs. Biddle from Four Corners who uses her cane to smash ankles and plough through crowds like Moses parting the Red Sea. Mrs. Biddle, who prays for the Apocalypse, for God's Cleansing Wrath. Egg shivers, thinking about the Ouiji board. Egg saw a picture of the frozen people of Pompeii in her *Young Reader's Guide to Science*. They were turned to stone, like Lot's wife. Did they look back? And what did they see? And then she thinks, what kind of God would do that?

She feels a sudden thrill of fear and wonders, maybe she is the one who is cursed. Maybe she is the one who is going to Hell.

Surrounded by heralding angels in Sunday school, by Jesus healing the Leapers, Egg thinks of all her sins. The mints from the drawer. The coins she pinches from her Mama's purse. All the lies she tells Papa. She thinks of Kuldeep, of a wrong wrong wrong she doesn't have a name for. She thinks of how she makes Mama sad, how she makes Kathy tired. She is useless. She is selfish. Egg slips her hand into her pocket, her fingers curling around the crumbled page, rubbing the rough sheet torn from the *Calgary Herald*. Now she is a vandal and a thief. Egg raises her hand and asks Mrs. MacDonnell, "If you do one thing bad, one thing, does it rub out all the good things you've done in your life?"

Egg has heard Mrs. MacDonnell say that to teach is a holy calling. Mrs. MacDonnell looks thoughtful. She takes out her handkerchief, white as dead lilies, and lays it on the table. "I'll leave it up to you to decide," she says and she raises her fountain pen and flicks it at the immaculate cloth. Black ink splatters the white. Droplets that stain and grow.

Mrs. MacDonnell holds up the handkerchief with the tips of her fingers. "What do you think? Wouldn't you say it's ruined?"

Egg looks at the blotted cloth. She says nothing but a part of her shrivels. Egg can feel the poison in what Mrs. MacDonnell has done, she can feel the mean and the ugly and she takes it inside her. Egg's soul is tainted, the inky blots growing. It's all there in front of her, there in black and white. White is good, white is holy, that's what Mrs. MacDonnell is saying. Egg thinks of Kathy, and her mother, her father, and Albert. Albert must be burning. When you fall, you burn.

Egg puts up her hand. She has to pee but instead of ducking into the washroom, she sneaks up the stairs. She can hear Reverend Samuels preaching his sermon through the thick oak doors of the vestibule. His words aren't clear but she can tell his voice is booming.

Egg turns towards the nave. The mural above the doors is of Isaac bound at the altar, Abraham's hand stayed by the angel. It's always spooky, that mural, like a test that no one can win.

The doors swing open and Raymond charges through, followed by Reverend Samuels's taunting to "Remember Romans and Leviticus! Let not the judgment of Sodom and Gomorrah be upon us!" The oak doors swing closed and Egg can see Raymond's face, his tears as he runs down the stairs and out the entrance of the church. It happens so fast, Egg doesn't know what to do. She wants to call out, Hey, Raymond, are you all right? Are you okay? But she doesn't.

Egg walks to the door and catches it before it closes. With one push she can see that the clouds have come in low and grey. Raymond weaves through the parking lot, stopping, finally, at his car door. A thin-shouldered boy with a mop of dark hair. She thinks he must be crying. Reverend Samuels's bark echoes harshly behind her. Bad, she feels it in her bones. Bad, like Martin Fisken's knuckle sandwich, like Glenda Wharton's pinches, the nail-crescent marks deep and bloody.

Egg doesn't understand. Raymond with his penguin dance, who tried to make her feel better. She looks up at the oak doors of the vestibule. No. This is wrong. But wrong against God means she is the Devil,

. . .

Later, in the afternoon, Egg rides out to the trestle bridge on her banana-seat bike, her hockey cards clicking through her spokes faster than a snake's rattle. She puts Evel on the railway tracks. She can feel the rumble through the steel and earth. The train is coming. Standing back, she waits as the engine approaches, the shrieking whistle that sets her teeth on edge, the quake all around as if the train were bursting through the air, rending the fabric of space, and Evel, on the track—she can't even hear the crack of plastic as the wheels roll over him.

The train thunders on, its speed deceptive, like some kind of lumbering beast. Egg crouches. She could almost touch it. Almost. She wonders at the momentum, such relentlessness. As the rumble in her blood drains away, the wind falls. *Chu-ga chug-ga*, the click-clack echoes across the plain.

Evel Knievel, split right in half.

She blinks back the dust in her eyes, her throat dry. Smoted, she thinks. Just like in the Bible.

Yes, she thinks. For Albert. Let the bad be over.

December

Christmas is coming, all the school a-carolling, Joy to the World, and Mr. Geary staggers from his office, reeking of liquor and Old Spice. He crashes into the lockers and everyone looks away. Because everyone knows, like the shiner Mrs. Ayslin sports after Christmas. She wears long sleeves throughout the year and no one ever says anything. Mama runs around the house with tinsel and bits of red and green, hauling out the tree from the attic and in the end she falls into the armchair with a glass of whiskey in her hand and a candy cane hooked over the rim. Everyone so fiercely, frantically jolly, Peace on Earth and Goodwill Towards Men. Egg wonders about the women, though, as Mrs. Ayslin wears sunglasses in the dead of winter. Mrs. MacDonnell says when you say men, you mean men and women but Egg is not so sure.

It is the last day before Christmas vacation and Egg wants to retrieve her Callard's candy tin (fruit drops), stuffed with buttons she has found, and pins, a hockey card of Bobby Orr creased at the edges, all stashed behind *William Shakespeare,*

The Complete Works. No one takes *The Complete Works*, it is way too heavy. It is late in the day so she must be cautious and the library will be closing early because of the Christmas pageant. Egg tries ducking under the counter but Miss Granger is too quick for her.

"Egg?"

Miss Granger has big eyes like the ostriches and pretty pretty lashes, only ostriches don't hide their heads in the sand. That is just a myth. When Egg looks up, Evangeline Granger's eyes go wide like she sees something, but then it's gone. She holds out a present, wrapped with a golden ribbon that bounces with curls. "Here you go, Egg. Merry Christmas."

Egg is surprised. She can only squeak out her thanks. She feels suddenly shy and flustered because she does not have a present for Evangeline.

Miss Granger smiles. "You can open it now, if you want to."

Egg pulls away the wrapping and holds a Thesaurus in her hands. It says in gold letters. It's a grown-up book, a hardcover.

"I've seen you with the dictionaries. I thought you might like a change. Do you know what that is?"

Egg opens the book. "It's a kind of dictionary for words that are extinct."

"Not quite." Miss Granger smiles, an odd twitch. Her hand reaches out, strokes down Egg's ruffled hair. Her smile slips and she retreats into her gingham. "It's for synonyms, words that mean the same thing."

"A whole book for that?"

"A whole book."

Egg stands for a moment, one foot pressed on the other. She feels a strong urge to hug her but thinks that Miss Granger would not allow it. Grown-ups have their separate rules, a language all their own.

"When I'm big, I'm going be a writer," Egg blurts, an offering of sorts.

"When you're big," Evangeline smiles, "but you can start small."

"I want to start when no one can tell me what to do." Her secret out, she bounces on her toes.

Evangeline smiles. "Good luck then."

Egg shuffles off, book in hand. At the door she pauses. "I'm going be a writer, just like Anne Frank."

Her face, Egg can't read her face. It's like Evangeline's smile has melted, like Egg has said something wrong. Egg wants to take it back but she doesn't know how to, she doesn't know what she has done. Egg closes the door behind her and in a moment she hears the buzz of the radio dial. Evangeline has her music, like Egg has her dictionary and there is no way they can talk to each other.

There is a boy in a plastic bubble. He lives there because he has no immunity. That means all the regular germs that float in the air can kill him, so he has to live inside some kind of barrier that the germs can't get into. It sounds sad because no one can hug him or touch him. Egg thinks that every one of us has a plastic bubble but it is invisible. We can't go inside each other; we don't know what someone else is thinking.

The boy in the plastic bubble is alone.

Egg stands in the hall, her hand on the door. She could go back into the library and say "Evangeline, I love you," or ask "Evangeline, why are you so sad?" but she can't because she is too afraid. She doesn't know why she is afraid. She holds the

Thesaurus in her hands but she doesn't have any answers. She thinks of the Moral of the Story, the brave knight battling the fierce dragon, the black and white of it. But real life is not like that. "Evangeline," she wants to say. "Evangeline?" she wants to ask her, but Egg stands, mute; she does not even have the words.

. . .

The Christmas pageant trots out the star, the manger, and a plastic Jesus (a Baby Blue Eyes) and almost all of Bittercreek crams into the school gym as if it is the Second Coming. Long tables line the walls of the gym, with baked goods, holiday baskets, the church raffle—all jostling for attention. The hockey team's in their tinfoil (Roman soldiers), the angel choir in their robes (bedsheets), and Principal Crawley pulls at his thin mustache. Egg's on the scaffold and she can see the entire town, the McDougalls, the Stubblefields, the Kennedys, and Gustafssons. She is not a part of the pageant because Mrs. Syms hand picks the angels and she is not among the chosen. On stage, the papier mâché star swings precariously over the Baby Blue Eyes. Evangeline is holding the props in her hands, as Mrs. Ayslin corrals the Three Wise Men for their entrance.

Tonight will be *Uncle Vanya*, with Stacey Norman and Jonathan Heap. Every year Mr. Parkinson stages *Our Town* for the Christmas play but since he ploughed his car into the stockyard, a Pabst Blue Ribbon bottle jammed beneath his brake pedal, Miss Chapman has stepped in with the Russians. Miss Chapman is swigging Mrs. Crawley's fresh eggnog, so innocent in a tiny Dixie cup. Mrs. Crawley is never skimpy when it comes to the rum, her flask tucked in her purse. Mrs.

Crawley is the wife of Principal Crawley, and even if her table is beside Reverend Samuels and the Bittercreek United Church she can do whatever she pleases.

Mrs. Biddles has a stack of Dixie cups in her hand. Egg takes note of this and thinks maybe it is best that Mama couldn't come. Rum is not her drink anyway.

Egg sees Miss — no, *Ms.* Chapman — by the door, her arms crossed, behind a cloud of smoke. Ms. Chapman's cigarette glows, like an all-seeing eye. Egg doesn't know what to make of Ms. Chapman. Ms. Chapman has come from Outside Bittercreek. Surely things must be done differently there. But Ms. Chapman saw Martin Fisken push little Jimmy Simpson from the swing set and she didn't even give him a glare. Didn't that say something about right and wrong? Egg thinks of all the bad things in the world. Maybe God is like that — a lunch monitor who doesn't really care.

From her perch on the scaffold, Egg can see Kathy and Stacey below her, by the girls' basketball table. They lean together, their foreheads almost touching. Egg scoots down and slips behind the curtain. It's not spying if you are just there, hiding from the bully gang. It's not spying if people talk so loud you can't help but hear.

Kathy groans. "It's like that *Twilight Zone* where the kid holds the entire town hostage and no one can get out."

"No, no, no. We're the one where everyone else is pig-ugly and no one understands that we're the beautiful people."

"We're still stuck until the end of the year."

Stacey lights up. "Then Paris. Or New York. Or—"

"Coal River. Or Calgary."

"We'll get out of here, Kathy. The scout from the east, maybe even a basketball scholarship — remember what Coach Wagner said."

Egg's ears prick up. What could they mean? Kathy leaving? But Mama and Papa... Egg feels like someone is standing on her chest.

Egg peeps out between the curtains. Stacey's hand is on Kathy's shoulder.

As she gazes across the auditorium, Egg catches sight of Pet Stinton and the townie gang by the edge of the assembly. Pet is staring at Kathy but Kathy doesn't see. Kathy and Stacey stand close, too close, and if Egg can see this, so can Pet Stinton. Kathy is not careful. Kathy is never careful.

Egg pops between Kathy and Stacey. "Martin's after me!" she cries, and she tells herself this is only half a lie. Martin is always after her. It's not like crying wolf at all.

Kathy looks around, bristling, as Stacey's arm slides around Egg. "Then you stay with us. You'll be safe." Egg catches the scent of Stacey's Love's Baby Soft.

With relief, Egg sees that Pet Stinton has turned her attention to the stage, to the Shepherd who has knocked over the Baby Jesus cradle and conked Mother Mary on her head with his curly staff.

For the rest of the pageant, the angels sing off-key, heralding the coming Kingdom as the papier mâché Bethlehem star crashes onto the stage. Mr. Jolean conducts his motley orchestra, his arms frantically windmilling in a desperate attempt to keep the chaos at bay, but Egg's thoughts are elsewhere. The scholarship, the end of high school for Kathy. And Stacey. The thought comes unbidden to her, of Reverend Samuels's last sermon, his fists slamming on the pulpit, quoting Leviticus and Romans. When Egg went into Gustafsson's for Kathy's Christmas surprise, she heard Mrs. Gustafsson say that Raymond was chased out of Bittercreek by Douglas Fisken and his gang.

The curtain falls and the lights come up to a collective sigh. Stacey must make her way backstage to the dressing rooms for her *Uncle Vanya*, where Kathy will be helping with the pulleys and winches. Egg watches Kathy follow Stacey to the stage. Stacey is pretty and kind, her shoes come all the way from Toronto from the Eaton's catalogue. Egg knows that Stacey is taking her sister away, away from her family, away from Bittercreek. She wants to call Kathy back but as she opens her mouth, she sees Martin Fisken by the edge of the steps. Egg tucks in her shoulders and runs — behind the stacked chairs, behind the pageant sign, down the long hallway, rushing past Miss Granger and Mrs. Ayslin who whisper by the fountain. A panic stitch digs into her side. Everything is changing too fast.

Egg rushes to the heavy outside doors, the big heave against her chest and her wince at the slap of air as they slam solidly behind her. The Chinook wind is warm against her face and she can see the arc of clouds above the horizon, the bare concrete and the balding patches of snow on the distant green.

The trees that line the street, so naked, claw at the sky.

Egg takes a deep breath.

The sky is big today. Sometimes Egg can feel it, the curly clouds and the wind, like something tugging at her, the push and pull of currents, something so big that can swallow her up, swallow her like she was nothing at all. Sometimes she can see it, chasing streaks across the sky. With a sky like this she can't help but want to spread her wings and fly.

She tries to think of how the world must look from Heaven, all blue and shiny, perfect even. From Heaven everything must seem just right, swirling clouds and green rainforests and sandy deserts all balanced together. But up close you see the ugly. Up close is where she lives.

Egg hears a metallic rattle from the edge of the schoolyard, like the scrape of an empty pop can when she crushes it on her heel, the drag against the hard pavement. The baseball diamond is empty; there is only the rustle of leaves caught in the mesh. But—Egg cocks her head. The echoey *tin tin rattle rattle* raises the hair on the back of her neck. Egg turns but they've already got her, two Mary-Margarets, one on each arm, and Chuckie grabs the scruff of Egg's neck. Her glasses are knocked askew. Her hand goes up to catch them but it is too late, she's lost them now. Her Mama will be so disappointed! Chuckie laughs, his breath smelling of sour peanut butter. Egg hates peanut butter. But that metallic rattle creeps up her spine. The sound unnerves her. What could it be?

Martin Fisken rolls the garbage can towards her. His grin is wide like the cat in that spooky story *Alice in Wonderland*. Martin does not even quicken his pace; he just casually kicks the dented can towards her. Egg twists. She tries to run but they've got her, her feet barely touch the ground. They toss her into the can, headfirst, thud against the bottom, a sharp pain on her head, like her brain splitting open, and then the world starts rolling.

Tumbling, her stomach heaves, the sky turning over, the grind of concrete and metal so loud, *bang bang bang* as they smack the tin, the sound booming inside her ears, from the back of her eyes, inside her brain. Her head hits the can, her hands scraping the metallic sides for some kind of hold. And the smell — that wet, sweet smell, so rotten — she feels that lurch in her stomach, that bitter acid burn in her throat.

"Egg?"

Kathy's voice, her arms reach out, she lifts Egg, holds her. Egg clings to her through a wave of dizziness, eyes spinning, clutch in her belly, clings to her as if she is the only solid thing in the whole entire universe, as Kathy gently picks the trash from Egg's hair, and wipes away the filth.

Kathy whispers in her ear, "It's all right, Egg. It's all right."

There's blood on the snap buttons and Egg leans down. Egg vomits, like something spilling out of her, the evil, the bad.

Kathy strokes her back.

"You're all right."

Egg can see Evangeline Granger walking towards them, and Mrs. Ayslin, in tears. Stacey comes behind them with a look on her face that tells Egg that something is really, really wrong. Her eyes sting. Egg wipes away the wet on her forehead, stares at the blood smeared on her hand, that shock of red. She grabs at her shirt, at the trash caked on her arm. She doesn't like it and brushes harder, then rougher, at the stains, the clinging rot. Egg is sobbing, the wet and the dirt and the smell. It will never come off her, she is tainted forever. Frantic, she clutches at herself but Kathy is there, holding her.

"You're all right. I've got you," Kathy murmurs, "I've got you."

Egg hides her face in Kathy's shoulder, as her sister picks her up and rocks her, away from all the prying eyes. She can feel the strength in her sister's arms, as Kathy scoops her up and takes her home.

. . .

Egg stands on the toilet seat, staring into the bathroom mirror. Her glasses are a little bent so she bares her teeth and lets out a pirate hiss—"Arghhh!" The cut above her eye has almost healed; she thinks she is more Cyclops than pirate but she doesn't know how a Cyclops sounds. Cyclops is from Greek mythology—their monsters are the best. They have hydras which are two-headed serpents but if you cut off one head, you get two more. In *D'Aulaires' Greek Myths*, Atlas holds up the sky, a punishment for his sins. The Gods give few rewards. You get to live and that's about it, she reckons. Maybe it's the thought that counts.

Monster means big. Monster means ugly. Monster means different. The Dictionary says that.

In the Greek myths, sometimes the monster was once a mortal who became horrible through a punishment. But that didn't solve the evil. It just made it huge. Maybe that's where all the bad comes from, Egg thinks, a bad so big that it bursts out of nowhere. And then she thinks of Papa, his exile in the ostrich barn. What bad did he do?

"Egg!" Kathy calls.

Egg runs down the stairs, grabs her jacket from the hook and bursts out the door. They are going to Calgary! She sees Kathy by the truck, already with her foot on the running board. Egg starts to sprint to the doors but she can't resist a spin. A blur of colours swirl around her. She marvels at the motion, as if she is in the centre of universe, a string pulled, a release into the whirlwind. The sky over Bittercreek, the clouds caught, like on a cotton candy stick—she points, wants to show Kathy, show the world—

"Come on, Egg," Kathy says, "we don't have forever."

Egg thinks, well, nobody has forever, and bounces onto the front seat. She taps her feet together: today she gets to sit shotgun.

They drive through flat fields, then turn as the fields slope and slouch into the distance. Egg gazes out the window. She sees a creeping blanket of snow begin to cover the slight crests, filling in the shallow dips; a line of fence posts makes an exclamation. Look, a snowshoe hare! Egg spots the fuzzy winter coat against a barren swatch of earth and thinks the feet aren't that big at all. The sheets of white cut starkly against an abrupt valley, the gash of a coulee. The sun is brilliant, a kaleidoscope light that bursts into three hovering beams. Kathy points out the sun dog, explaining how light passing through ice crystals (Kathy calls them diamond dust) makes that magical halo. Hexagonal, Egg must look that up in the dictionary. They drive over fields and fields — then over the hump — they can see strip malls and streets. As they wind their way into downtown Calgary, over the Bow River, towards the concrete needle that Kathy calls the Husky Tower.

Passing the trolley buses on Eighth Avenue, Kathy pulls into the parking lot and Egg can barely sit still. On the street, Egg runs past the window displays, into Eaton's, straight to the toy section. She can see the box, the Six Million Dollar Man action figure with the Bionic eye and fold-back skin for his Bionic arm.

Egg glances behind her. Kathy leans over the glass case in the jewellery section, her eyes caught by all the glitter. The saleswoman behind the counter pulls out a silver box with a flourish. Inside, a golden heart locket on a velvet pillow.

No no no, Egg thinks. All the songs say never to give your heart away. Nancy Sinatra sings "Bang Bang" on the radio and that is when Egg knows that if they can come for Raymond, they can come for Kathy too.

. . .

It is Christmas Eve and Egg wants to fly. She wants invisibility and an X-O-skeleton, super-strength, and X-ray vision. Egg wants to eat Lucky Charms for breakfast. She wants a family that eats dessert. She wants snap buttons and overalls and a jackknife and slingshot but she wouldn't use it against animals because that would be wrong.

But most of all she doesn't want to be Egg anymore.

She thinks of the carollers on Maple as they go from door to door, the lights that line Main, the glow of red, green, and yellow. Bittercreek, sprinkled with a trace of snow, like fairy dust, must look like the picture-perfect holiday card.

Mama slumps over the kitchen table. At her feet, the bottle rolls in ever smaller circles. Egg chews her lip. She doesn't like the sound of the glass against the floor, that hollow hollow sound. Kathy's out with Jillian and Debbie and she's been grumpy because Stacey's with her cousins in Ontario. No one talks about Raymond, and that's when Egg knows that he is gone for good.

But Mama's here. Papa won't come out from the ostrich barn so it's all up to her.

Egg bites her knuckles and starts with armadillo and cheats with narwhal but x—she can't think of any animal that starts with x.

It's not fair. She's too small to know what to do. If Kathy

were here...but then Kathy spent the day sweeping out the ostrich barn with Papa. In the first year, when the ostriches went blind, Kathy swept them out every day before school and even after basketball practice during the finals.

Mama kicks the bottle with her foot, snorting against the table. When she turns her head, Egg can see the line of the checkered placemat against her mother's cheek.

Hollow hollow.

She tries to get Mama up but grown-ups are so heavy. Mama's words slide into each other. The liquor has her, she's drowning in it.

"Mama!" Egg shakes her, the shot of fear making her bold. "Mama!"

Mama's eyes flicker open. Her mouth gapes. Egg wrinkles her nose at the smell.

"Come on, Mama. Let's go upstairs."

They stagger to the doorway, in the darkness of the alcove. Mama's hip hits the china bureau and Egg can hear the tinkling. Twilight scattered by crystal, the glass surfaces glinting darkly.

Mama staggers. Egg feels like she is slipping through her fingers. She tries, she does, but Mama's too heavy. They slide to the floor.

The train whistle calls from a thousand miles away.

"Osamu," Mama slurs, "the sirens..."

Egg is scared that Mama doesn't know her.

"Go to sleep, Mama," Egg whispers. Mama rolls on her back, her mouth open. Egg goes to the living room and takes the comforter off the back of the big chair. At least Egg can wrap the blanket around her.

Mama's mouth is open and Egg doesn't want it to be open. She doesn't want to stay beside her and she's afraid to go away.

"What's the use of it? What's the point?" Her Mama's voice rings with a sudden clarity. "At least your father..." but she trails off and Egg can't catch any of it.

Egg sits in the dark. She can hear beyond the creaking walls of the house, beyond the fields, and far, far, far away from Bittercreek. A coyote howls from the south field. She thinks of flying, up to the sky and beyond. In space there is no sound. Egg wonders how that must feel, so far and so alone. The blue whale, she thinks, or animal alphabets. Mama sleeps. Egg lays her head on Mama's shoulder, listens to her mother's beating heart. She doesn't want to leave Mama but she must remember for the notebook. Osamu. Osamu. And the sirens.

Egg sleeps. When she wakes she is snug under her blanket, tucked into her bed. The moonlight falls across her bed, an unearthly blue. The sirens, she remembers but the name has slipped from her lips, and is gone.

. . .

On Christmas morning Egg wakes to the smell of cinnamon. She thinks that Albert and Kathy must be downstairs with Mama making the Christmas pancakes. They always have pancakes on Christmas morning, Albert whipping the cream into a frothy peak in the big bowl. And presents! This year she wants a Six Million Dollar Man action figure with a Bionic eye you could actually look through and—

Then Egg remembers about Albert. This is the first Christmas without him.

On the stairwell, she peers through the bars of the banister. Kathy is in the kitchen, making the Christmas pancakes. In the living room the tinsel glints on the tree, the presents are tucked under the pine branches.

Egg shuffles into the kitchen and sits at the table. Kathy turns at the scrape of the chair against the floor.

"I thought you'd be up by now." Kathy flips the pancakes. "Merry Christmas!"

"Where's Mama?"

"Oh, she's just sleeping in a little."

Egg can see the furrow in Kathy's brow.

"I made your favourite—pancakes with chocolate chips!" Kathy adds. This chirping, cheery Kathy unnerves Egg. She wants her brooding big sister back.

"Can we do the presents before breakfast?"

"Sure, don't see why not."

Egg runs to the tree, to colourful boxes spread under the branches. She zeros in on the big red box with the tag *To Egg, From Santa* and tears open the wrapping, too impatient for the ribbon. She stares at the package.

It is a Big Jim action figure.

"Look, he has a karate board and a baseball. There's even a dumbbell and muscle band. See, there's a button on his back," Kathy says, pointing at the box. "You can actually break the karate board. And he throws the baseball too."

Egg stares at the package. The Six Million Dollar Man has a Bionic Power Arm with grip action. He has special skin on his arm that can roll back, revealing his Bionic parts. Kathy looks expectant so Egg says, "Gee thanks. It's just what I wanted."

"Well, it's from Santa."

Then Egg knows that it's Kathy who bought the presents. Mama is gone. For her there is no Christmas without Albert.

Egg hugs the box to her chest. "It's the best present ever, Kathy."

Kathy holds out another gift. "Here, this is from me." She hands Egg the rectangular package.

The red wrapping falls away to a book with lined pages. "It's a journal, like Anne Frank's," Kathy explains. "And here," she pulls out a small rectangular box.

Egg opens the hinged lid. "A fountain pen! Thanks Kathy."

Egg remembers her present for Kathy, sitting under her bed. She runs up to her bedroom and grabs the big square box, as big as her head, wrapped in foolscap that she borrowed from Mrs. Syms's desk after she slapped the blackboard brushes. Egg ordered the present from Gustafsson's General Store, no treats and candies for three whole months, she had saved all her allowance for this one gift. She runs down the stairs and she places the box in Kathy's hands. Breathless, she feels the flutter in her chest rising.

Kathy delicately peels away the wrapping and lifts the ball out of the box: an official Spalding NBA basketball, with a squiggly signature, and the logo of the player running down the court. Egg watches as her sister rolls the ball from hand to hand, how she measures its weight. Kathy bounces the ball, feels it true, grips the pebbled surface of the leather, traces the rubber seam with her thumb.

Egg can feel her sister's stillness. The surface that seems almost to crack. Egg says, "It's for when the scout comes…" She doesn't add, "for when you go away."

Kathy hugs her. Egg feels the tremor in Kathy's chest, the ragged breath that she draws in. She thinks of Albert, crowing at the top of the stairs, his voice booming through the house, his present, the pickup truck that will smash into the train by the railway trestle. Merry Christmas, Egg whispers silently, to her big sister Kathy who is always taking care of her. Egg bites her lip. She wants so much to tell her that she loves her but they are not that kind of family. So she wishes for her sister's happiness. Big sister Kathy, who has made so many sacrifices. Merry Christmas.

. . .

All day *Happy Days*, *Gilligan's Island*, even a rerun of *The Buck Shot Show*. Kathy makes Jiffy Pop on the stove. Egg watches the aluminum rise, the flat pan growing into a glittering ball, all in a clatter of popping kernels, impossibly, right before her eyes.

Jiffy Pop, the real miracle, right before *The Brady Bunch*, and Canada Dry, straight from the bottle. The champion of ginger ales. It says so, right on the bottle.

Egg thinks that *The Brady Bunch* is the best family ever. There is a dead mama and a dead papa but that doesn't matter anymore because now the live mama and live papa have found each other. There are three boys and three girls and a maid called Alice, on a staircase that holds them all together. Everything is perfect, perfect, and it's not like anyone died after all.

When Kathy takes out Papa's dinner tin, *The CBS Evening News* comes on with Walter Cronkite. There is something comforting about the sameness of Walter, his drooping mustache, the dull anchor desk. But a report comes through on Cyclone Tracy. Christmas Day Cyclone Tracy rips through Darwin,

Australia, killing over seventy people and destroying much of the city. Egg sits, surrounded by the scattered bits of brightly coloured bows and wrapping paper, watches the newsreel. Merry Christmas, she thinks, Merry Christmas. On the newsreel, the smashed buildings and flipped cars look like Lego and dinky cars. Egg holds Big Jim on her lap. Big Jim has a button on the back that flexes his arm into a karate chop. Slap slap, slap slap. A toy that plays at being a superhero.

Smash, smote, smash.

On the news they call it an Act of God. Most of Darwin destroyed. But they should have known, shouldn't they? Like some kind of test, like Job in the Bible. The survival of the fittest. Or a punishment like the Flood and the plagues of Egypt. Job had it tough though, boils and everything. His family smoted—just like that.

Later, in the crawl space, above the ostrich pens, Egg takes the forbidden matches and melts Big Jim's karate chop. She watches the transformation, the drip drip of plastic. That harsh burnt smell curls in her nostrils. She wraps the arm in a fold of tissue, for Kathy must never know, she would never understand. A sacrifice. For the souls of Darwin, Australia.

January 1975

engine engine number nine
going down chicago line
if the train goes off the tracks
do you want your money back?
yes or no

Egg balances on the rail and walks the track, her arms stretched out, as if in flight. The railway tracks, running side by side, look as if they're going to meet in the distance but Egg knows this is an optical illusion. That's when something looks like something but it's not. The world is full of optical illusions. Like the colour of the sky and the colour of the ocean. Water and air don't have a colour. Blue is an illusion and an illusion is fake.

But Egg wonders, how can a colour be fake?

Fake is not true even if it is real. It's like doing a magic trick but you know the quarter just falls into your lap. It's there but it's a lie.

And lies are bad.

The wind blows harsh, a clipper that could blow you into the ass-end of Saskatchewan, and clouds roll across the sky like tumbleweeds. Egg lifts her head high. Ostriches stargaze, their heads bent back. They twirl and make the whole earth spin.

"Cumulus nimbus!" Egg shouts because in fact, they are.

Anne Frank is in New York City working as a telephone operator but now Kathy tells her that she's on Broadway, sure to be a star. Egg thinks "Over the Rainbow," even if the flying monkeys scared the bejesus out of her and who'd want to leave all those colours for washed-out Kansas anyway?

Egg thinks of the draw of the well, that strangely comforting darkness. She thinks of the whispers from the television after Mama has fallen asleep in the big chair. Sins and salvation, the world so clear, Heaven and Hell parted like the Red Sea, the exodus from the Pharaoh's Army to the milk and honey of the Promised Land.

That story. There's no place like home.

She breaks out into a full run. Twice around the barn, all the way to the haystack. She pants, her lungs filling with the frigid air. The ground is frost-hard, ungiving, but Egg will not stop. She is in training. She has a plan. *Mutual of Omaha* says that every animal has a niche, a place in the cycle of life. There is an ecosystem, a balance to it all. A place for everyone and everyone in their place. That's God's great plan and she can be a part of it too.

Popular is the best. There is Cool Pop, Pretty Pop, but best of all is Jock Pop. There is no Smart Pop because Brainer is something else altogether. This spring she will try out for the baseball team, just like Albert. That will be her niche. A niche is so you can fit in.

Egg sees that Jack Henry has pulled up to the barn with his silver gooseneck trailer. He towers over Papa at the gate. Jack Henry is their neighbour on the west side, tall and thin, with a grizzled beard that keeps on growing. A veteran of the Second World War, his left arm ends in a stump below the elbow. Egg is fascinated by that stump. You would think that Papa and Jack Henry would hate each other as Mr. Henry lost his hand in the Pacific but there they stand, Mr. Henry with his chewing tobacco and Papa with his tea. There used to be Saturday hooch in the barn but since Albert's death, Papa just nods a good night and Jack Henry twirls the corner of his beard and shifts from foot to foot.

Egg ducks behind the house as they hitch the ramp to the end of the last pen. She watches as the chicks—no, they are juveniles and yearlings now—are corralled into the corner of the outer pen, their heads covered by socks with the ends cut off. They stand sturdy, eyes sheathed and mollified by these tubes, easily led up the trailer ramp. Egg can see their feathers, their bobbing heads through the slats but she can't see Esmeralda. She watches Papa recheck the count and sign off on Jack Henry's sheet.

Jack Henry's voice is low and slurring but Egg catches, "You gotta live for something," as his one good hand clutches the door. Jack Henry is a solid man. He adds, "At least, that's what they say." With a grunt, he climbs into his truck and pulls away.

When the trailer turns onto the road, Egg runs to the barn. The hatch box and the chick crate are gone, the third pen is empty. The six breeders are still in their coops. Egg sits on the stool by the wooden stove and swings her legs. Her toes do not even graze the floor.

Esmeralda is gone. There is no Charlotte to save her.

Papa opens the gate and with two deliberate stomps, he kicks off the dirt, the clinging snow. As he reaches for the broom, Egg knows that he has seen her.

She clears her throat. "I thought, maybe, she was too small to send away."

Her father makes short even strokes with the broom. He picks out words like stones from the feed. "You know, I grew up by the zoo in my town, saw all kinds of animals — tigers, lions, bears. It was like all the world was in that place. The elephants were the best. The smartest. But big. They'd eat out of your hand and one of them, he'd snatch your cap, if you weren't careful. Him, I called Tetsuro."

Egg looks up. "He was your favourite?"

"Yes." Papa holds the broom close, pressing down with his palms. "See, they had this gap in the fence, behind, where they dumped all the manure and I'd go every day after school. Well, when they had school. When the war came, I didn't have much use for school. I was as old as you are now. It was nasty, that. They had to kill all the animals, you know, in case a bomb, in case they escaped. That was a real shame. They poisoned all of them and they died. But the elephants, it's as if they knew that the food was poisoned. So they didn't eat it."

Egg blinks. "What happened to them?"

Papa clears his throat, the broom very still. "They starved. It took a long time for them to starve." Papa places the broom by the tool box. "I always wanted to raise elephants but there's no money in it. You know ostriches — there's feathers, and meat, and oil, and raising chicks for breeders. It brings the money in. Sometimes you got to do hard things and make sacrifices. It's the way of life. You'll understand when you're older."

"Yes, Papa. I know."

Egg scoots off the chair and into the house. In her room, she huddles beneath her sky-blue blanket, as if under a field of stars. She will look up elephants in her *Young Reader's Guide to Science*. Elephants never forgive, that's what Egg remembers.

. . .

Egg watches Kathy hold court, the basketball in her hands. On her game, Kathy is all fluid motion, as if attached to the ball by an invisible thread. Coach Wagner shouts from the sidelines as Kathy weaves and bobs, cutting down the stretch, feint and pass, and the shot against the backboard, sailing through the hoops no questions asked. The Bittercreek Eagles look a fine sight in their dark blue uniforms. Kathy's number, thirty-four, is stitched in gold. Last week, after basketball practice, Kathy had taken Egg onto the court, explaining the geometry of the perfect shot, the jump and the setup.

Kathy knows these kinds of things; her head is full of basketball. The next Olympics, the Montreal Olympics, will feature the first women's basketball competition. On her shelf, Kathy has a picture of Noel MacDonald of the Edmonton Grads — clipped from the *Edmonton Herald* — her winning streak that no one has ever broken. Beside her, Wataru "Wat" Misaka, the first Japanese ever in the NBA.

Egg tries very hard to follow the line of the throw. Kathy says Euclid, all angles, all focus. Ever since the garbage can incident, Kathy drives her to school and back, so Egg watches her sister's practice. Egg likes watching Kathy run down the court, the ball a natural extension of her body, how she wills the trajectory of the bumpy rubber ball, the dash and scatter of her teammates.

There are granny shots and banana cuts, you can drop a dime, or shoot from downtown. Egg, hidden beneath the bleachers, thinks about the basketball scholarship, the scout from the east.

There, by the team bench, Stacey cheers after Kathy sinks a layup. Egg sees Kathy blush. Not everyone has their own private cheerleader.

The whistle blows as Coach Wagner calls for a huddle at the bench. Egg ducks under the back seats. She scans the court and sees Pet Stinton in her bright pink Pilgrim pumps with silver buckles that sparkle like town.

Petunia Stinton walks over to Stacey, who draws her arms up in front of her chest. Pet Stinton, who is the queen bee of the senior year, Pet Stinton, whose father owns half the town. Even Egg can see that Pet Stinton is fake in the most dangerous way.

Stacey nods her head and smiles at Petunia's words but her arms seem stiff, her shoulders rigid. Stacey's smile wanes, as Pet chatters and waves to the court. Egg watches as Stacey tries to turn away but Pet seems to hold her, leaning in at an angle, pushing away with a mocking laugh. Egg thinks of the *Mutual of Omaha's Wild Kingdom*, the hooded cobra who weaves and rises before the fatal attack.

The bell rings and Coach Wagner dismisses the team. They come together in one cheer, hands clasped, then scatter, arms raised. When Egg looks back to Stacey, Pet Stinton is gone.

Egg taps her feet together.

Ostriches don't hide their heads in the sand. That is a myth. They lay their heads down on the ground, using their camouflage and hope for the best. They are born runners, with long, agile legs and they can deliver a mean kick. Kathy is strong and smart, good at sports and science, but Pet Stinton still lords over them all. Egg can't wrap her head around the schoolyard jungle. Still, Egg thinks, you don't want to corner an ostrich. Even lions will think twice with that claw.

In the parking lot, Egg climbs into the truck and slides between the front seats to the rear bench. She stretches out. Kathy and Stacey take the front seats; Stacey always rides shotgun when Kathy drives.

"What the hell?" Kathy swears, jumping up from her seat. A plastic Jesus flies by Egg's ear but she only ducks beneath the collar of her puffy coat. As they pull out of the lot, Egg feels the bump of the curb. The road rolls beneath her as the cab rocks, gently, the back fishtailing onto the main road. The dusk has fallen, winter gloom. Egg closes her eyes.

"You should have seen her face!" Stacey's voice breaks through the bubble in Egg's brain. Clear, with a wonderful lilt, Stacey's laughter fills the space like a burst of wildflowers, like confetti. Egg feels a shift, as her body slides on the back bench from the pull of the turn. They must be on the flats near Stacey's place. Egg is almost dozing, but perks up as Stacey quietly asks, "Have you thought about it?"

Egg thinks her words sound like a wish thrown into a well.

"Hm?" Kathy's eyes are on the road.

"Graduation. Life after Bittercreek." An edge of impatience rides Stacey's voice.

Egg opens her eyes just a smidgen.

"Not really. Things have been kind of crazy. Dad wants a new pen for the next season and Mama's—"

"Things will always be crazy," Stacey blurts. The falling snow has turned to ice—Egg can hear the crackle of the pellets against the cab's roof, above the rumble of the engine.

"You're going to stay." Stacey sighs, her shoulders slumping.

Through the glow of dashboard, Kathy's hand reaches for Stacey.

But Stacey shakes her head, her voice rising. "I don't want to die here. I don't want to scrub the same floor for the rest of my life or talk about how hard the meatloaf is, or bitch about ring-around-the-collar. I want to meet people—people who don't know who my parents are, who haven't known me since I was ten. Do you know what I mean? Kathy. I want to be new."

The ice pellets. Egg's hand on the vinyl seat. She feels the gentle hum of the drive.

They drive in silence. At Stacey's driveway, Kathy stops the truck, her hand wrestling awkwardly with the clutch. The engine spins down with a thud. Egg feels it in her chest.

They sit.

"You can't stay and I can't leave," Kathy says. "I can't leave Egg."

"The town's dying," Stacey's voice is full of tears, "you stay and it'll bury you."

In the space between them, Egg can see the windshield, the stars, glittering cold and hard. Orion, she thinks, the Hunter.

Stacey leans, kisses Kathy's cheek, and Egg closes her eyes tight. *Aardvark, bat, cougar, dingo. D* is danger. Dark. Death. Doom.

The door slams, shudders through the cab of the truck.

Stacey is gone.

Kathy sits. Behind her, Egg is frozen, her ears burning. She can see the rigid set of her sister's shoulders, how she grips the steering wheel. Egg cannot reach out for her, she cannot say a word.

Kathy starts the engine and pulls off the drive. Egg can feel the gravel, thrown up by the tires. She looks out the window.

The moon is following them.

. . .

Winter rain is the worst. The cold, the wind, and the stinky wet boots.

Egg stands in the lunchroom, studying the droplets as they hit the window. She stares at the meandering beads, how they slowly gather into reluctant streaks, abruptly merging into rivulets, faster and faster — then the final plummet to the ground. She tries to think of the water cycle: evaporation, precipitation... but her brain feels stuck. She feels thick and soggy. She rubs her forehead against the cool glass. Even her blinks are slow.

Grey day, grey day.

Egg yawns. Cloudy head.

Martin Fisken is sick today, so Egg will take the stormy weather. Like the song. Mama loves that song.

In her *Young Reader's Guide to Science* there are stories of Archimedes in his bathtub, Newton with his apple. In her book Egg has read about the honeybees, their dance to tell you where the nectar is. That's their language. They have a queen and something called Hive Mentality. Kathy tells her to always be careful of Hive Mentality.

A sudden gust lashes rain against the glass and Egg almost jumps back from the window.

Outside the sky darkens. Egg can see the reflection of the lunchroom in the window: Stacey, in a splash of vibrant red, sitting by Jonathan Heap's side in the Fisken/Stinton circle at one table. Her hand so casually loops his elbow. Jonathan Heap, a thin, quiet boy, cousin to the vile Petunia Stinton, son to Heap's Hardware on Main Street.

Kathy, alone, at her own table, in a bubble of shock.

Oh no.

Later that night Kathy is on the telephone, her voice urgent, at times breaking, looping the phone cord through her fingers, over and over, the restless twirl and drop.

Egg crouches under the kitchen table, watching her sister pace. She tucks her knees up under her chin. Her Mama stands at the kitchen sink, her hands in the sudsy water. How still her Mama is. How silent, as she soaks the dishes, as she eavesdrops on Kathy in the living room. Egg traces the speckles in the linoleum. Her Mama knows what is happening, that Kathy loves Stacey, that Stacey is gone. But Mama believes in Jesus. Egg wants so much to ask about Leviticus and Romans, of God's love in Darwin, Australia.

The door slams. Egg turns to see Kathy through the door window, turning up her collar, rushing into the night.

"*Shikata ga nai*," her mother sighs.

Egg remembers her parents at the kitchen table, their voices low, the sky a wraparound cloak of twilight. Japanese is the talk of the midnight table. English is to fit in. Japanese is only her father's occasional *ahra-ma*, a sigh and a mutter, a code that Egg does not understand.

She must write this down but her notebook is in her room. She runs upstairs.

At her mother's bedroom, she pauses. The door is slightly ajar. Egg can see the dark blue curtains that frame the frost-tinted window. Her hand presses lightly against the worn right panel and the door swings open. A heavy mahogany dresser with a three-panelled mirror sits to her left with a clutter of small fluted bottles of azure and emerald on the tray. It is the mirrors that draw her into the room, their reflections of the screen by the closet, that odd angle of the side table. Egg turns. The bed seems so large. Egg remembers bouncing on the *moufu*, that falling that is almost flying, a game of trampoline.

On the side table, there is a picture of Albert, Kathy, Papa, Mama, and Egg, a snapshot from their visit to the Japanese Garden in Lethbridge. It was only last fall that they were walking across the wooden bridge, gazing at the stone garden. Egg remembers the sculpted pines, the bell that rang so clear, the teahouse, golden yellow cypress — how the space lit up the second the sun shone through! Egg stares at the photograph. She can see Mama's dust trail on the picture frame, her fingertips against the glass.

In Lethbridge they had stopped at Nakashima's Japanese Food and Sundries. At least once a year, Papa would stop by Nakashima's but this was the first time that Egg had gone along. She wandered the aisles—all the names she could not understand. Lethbridge, with so many Japanese-Canadian beet farmers, because of the war. The ghost war, the one you don't read in history books, the shadow war with words like "evacuation," "work camps," and "internment." The war you know, but you never hear, the whispers of grown-ups as they turn away.

With her fist, Egg brushes away the dust, and places the picture back on the table. She shifts, her toe hitting—something. Beneath the table, she finds the box.

Her Mama's *tansu*. The scored dark wood, with dented iron plates on the corners and edges, black metallic handles that curve and swoop. The chest is as long as her arm, as deep as an ostrich egg.

A secret in a box.

Egg opens the lid.

A tin of Sakuma Drops in the corner, beside a wooden toy train and an old ticket stub. Egg picks up the tin and shakes it: empty. Tucked in the side, almost out of view, between a brown sheet of carefully folded, almost translucent paper, there is a black and white photograph, creased at the edges.

Egg draws out the sheet. It is so old she can feel the fibres of the page clinging to her fingertips like grains of sand. The paper falls away. The photograph is stiff, a dry glossy card that has lost its sheen, an image that has yellowed with age.

In the photograph there is a girl that looks like Mama, but like a young Mama, young as Egg, and a boy like Albert but it can't be Albert because how can Albert be older than Mama? Behind them, there is a train station with a crowd of men in uniforms—soldiers, Egg thinks—and a big burst of steam by the engine. Flags wave, caught in their frenzy, and the glint of metal, a white hot light on the shoulders of the men. Albert, no, not Albert, the one like Albert, he stands close to Mama as if to shield her from the frantic crowd.

The war, Egg thinks.

In the movies, war is about big men with big guns and words so twisted that their meaning is lost. Egg can't figure it out. Even the Dictionary is no help. In the movies the baby-faced boy dies and even if they say that war is bad, you can't help looking at all the explosions. Die die die. They play war in the schoolyard. But this photograph is not about bombs, or guns, or tanks or planes. Her Mama is scared and everyone is saying goodbye.

But the boy? Where is he now?

Egg takes the wooden train and climbs onto the bed. She stretches it out before her, up to the overhead light. She feels the bounce on the mattress like the rocking of a railcar. She can just make out the writing, carved into the side of the train as she bounces. Bounce, bounce, bounce—

"Egg!" Mama cries from the doorway.

Egg jerks, she falls from the bed. Her hands clutch the train —*crack*—as she snaps it in two.

Mama stares at her.

Egg tastes the blood: she has bitten her tongue.

"Get out!" her Mama screams, towering over her. Her eyes are hard and her voice—Egg has never heard her voice like that before.

Egg runs to her room and scuttles under the bed. In her panic she has run with the train that she has snapped. She stares at it. She has broken it. She has broken the family.

Snow

Snow

Snow

The evening falls yet the clouds are still luminous, holding twilight. The windows of the barn glow golden, the snowflakes caught in the halo.

Hello world. Egg taps her fingers against the glass.

Egg sits in her room, gazing out her window. She places her palm against the glass and breathes, frosting the pane.

She takes her hand away. Her print. Not a shadow, not a silhouette.

What is that?

A sign.

She will begin her practice today. She has been weak. She has been silly. She will start again for the test is soon to come. Like Job. Like the survival of the fittest.

She has to bring Mama out of the well. The whale has swallowed her, like Jonah. She doesn't know quite how to do it but she will find a way. Trial and error, they say. Practice makes perfect.

. . .

Kathy reads the current events in *The Globe and Mail* shipped in just for her, ever since Egg can remember. Kathy's current events are not so current—she picks up the stack on Saturday and reads the week all in one sitting. Something called "Watergate" in big black letters, along with "Vietnam." Watergate is in a place called Washington, and Vietnam is the war that has gone on forever. It's all on the six o'clock news, right after *Gilligan's Island*, and it's a far-away-ever-after that burns and burns and burns.

The photograph is in *The Globe and Mail*. It is an old photo, taken on June 8, 1972, outside the small village of Trang Bang, twenty-two miles outside Saigon. It is a picture of a country road, cropped fields on either side, smoke obscuring the grey distance. The photograph is not just the road, nor the field, nor the soldiers but the children, running, screaming, and at the centre, the girl, naked and burning. For Egg, an unfamiliar word: *napalm*.

After school, she decides that she will not wait for the end of Kathy's basketball practice. Egg will make her own way home. The road will be enough.

There are prairie tall tales, storms that pancake houses, a truck thrown into a tree, cows frozen milking ice cream, and ducks that fly away with a slough. The wind, however, is no joke and Egg shivers as she walks.

She stuffs her gloves on top of two fence posts by the Morgan's lot, a goodbye-hello and how-dee-do that bleakens the relentless white. Pinch your eyes to crush the glare. The air is brittle, Egg thinks. Her breath freezes, a cloud on her lips.

Here, on the road outside Bittercreek, the two fence posts, with the world in retreat, the horizon receding like an early-morning dream. The snow, the sky, the storm, the sudden, muffled quality of the air.

She slides out of her coat. This, too, she can leave behind.

Egg picks up a mound of snow with her bare hands, feeling the bite, the burn against her skin. The crystals melt, dissolving. *Metamorphosis.*

Again and again, she plunges her hands into the snowbank. White mitts.

It doesn't hurt at all, no. It doesn't hurt at all.

. . .

Kathy finds her, a mile from the house. Egg gives no clear answers as she is bathed and then bundled. Kathy sits her in the kitchen, surrounded by buckets of hot water, beneath a mountain of blankets. There is not a word about the lost coat and mittens.

Egg can't quite feel her ears but she tells no one.

Egg counts one-one-thousand, two-one-thousand. It is a trick that Kathy taught her, to tag the thunder to that electric flash, distance and velocity, the speed of sound to light. Egg blinks back the steam and readies herself but Kathy only pulls up a chair and settles in.

"You going to tell me, Egg?"

"What?"

Kathy rubs her eyes, the furrow between her brows deepening. "Why?"

"Dunno." The mist from the buckets fog Egg's glasses as they slide down. Nose sweat.

"Nekoneko was worried." Kathy's eyes chase the shadows in the china bureau. "Nekoneko was alone."

Egg clutches the stuffed cat in her arms, one-eyed Kitty who never blinks. "I was practising."

"What?"

"For the march from Auschwitz."

Egg holds herself, like the bolt before the strike. One-one-thousand, two-one-thousand, but Kathy only says, "You could have frozen to death."

"Who is Osamu?"

Now it is Kathy's turn to hold. "Who told you that name?"

Egg shrugs.

Kathy sighs. "Mama's brother. He died in the war."

It all goes back to the war.

"Kathy?"

"Yeah?"

"Mama's stuck in bed because of me," Egg says simply.

Kathy looks tired. "No, Egg, it's because... after Christmas..." Kathy sighs. "Go up and say hello."

Egg shuffles to the stairs and looks back at her sister. Kathy is as close to grown-up as you can get. Bossy-the-cow Kathy who thinks she knows everything. Grown-ups never tell you the whole story. They never tell you that dead is the old cat rotting in the copse with maggots rolling around in the eyes; they give you stories of angels and puffy-cloud Heaven. Grown-ups lie. They give you bits and pieces, they say "look how pretty" even when it is not — and then they make you smile over a lie that you know isn't the whole truth.

Egg hovers over the threshold of Mama's doorway. Ever since Egg broke the train, Mama gazes blankly at the walls. Not even the whiskey will get her up. It's like a staring contest where no one wins.

I was only trying to help, Egg thinks, but now I've made it worse.

"Mama?" Egg whispers, "I'm home." She thinks of Anne, in the Secret Annex. Margot was the mother's favourite daughter, smart, prim, and perfect.

She searches her mother's face for some kind of recognition. Mama's face against the white sheets is so deathly pale. Egg knows that the speed of light is the fastest ever, that the blue whale roams the seas, filling the oceans with song. She knows that Anne Frank sings on Broadway and that God smited

Darwin, Australia. Her Mama's like an iceberg, broken and drifting. Most of all, with that look, Egg knows that Mama hates her.

. . .

In geography, Egg learns that there are seven continents: North America, South America, Europe, Australia, Africa, Asia, and Antarctica. Mrs. Syms says continents are land masses but Europe and Asia — shouldn't they be one whole continent? Egg has some questions but she knows that Mrs. Syms does not like questions. Egg smooths out the map. It takes up her entire desk. A map is a wondrous thing. Why, you could walk from China to Portugal, from Portugal to the very bottom of Africa! What about a railroad? From the Yukon to the Patagonias! In front of her like this, it is as if you could jump from Calgary to Vancouver. Edmonton is a fingernail away.

As she colours in all the blue, someone smacks her elbow and the crayon scrawls into Greenland.

"Hey!" Egg looks up.

Martin stands beside her, all smiles, like a jack-in-the-box monkey.

At lunchtime, Egg slips into her empty classroom. She carefully peels her single slice cheese from the plastic wrapper and places the sticky slab onto Martin's chair. She hates the single slice. Sweaty cheese. With a glance at the clock, she hides behind her coat, which hangs from her hook at the back of the classroom. Her backpack covers her feet. This is the perfect disguise. Camouflage. Just like in the *Mutual of Omaha's Wild Kingdom*.

The bell rings and her stomach is jello.

As the class tumbles in, Egg peeks through her sleeve. She sees Martin take his seat. When Mrs. Syms strolls into the classroom and faces the blackboard, Egg slips to her desk.

At the end of the class, Martin stands and it is Glenda who points and says, "Eww, cheese butt!"

The class bursts out laughing. Egg watches as the tips of his ears turn red, burning down like a fuse until his face is flush in anger.

Martin catches her smiling.

His teeth are bared and Egg thinks, oh no.

At recess, Egg runs to the parking lot, quick-quack-quick, ahead of Martin. She hides behind the stunted bushes, tucks, makes herself small, her teeth chattering.

At the parking lot exit, Mrs. Ayslin and her husband push out the big doors that slap so heavy behind you. Mrs. Ayslin looks about to cry, her face crumbling behind her dark glasses. Mr. Ayslin's burly hand grips Mrs. Ayslin's arm too tight, pushing her to the car. Egg can see his teeth when he speaks, his lips curling as if he is about to swallow her whole, his whole body *shove shove shove*, his whole body *wrong*. Something is pressing at the back of Egg's eyes, a roar that fills up her ears. Mr. Ayslin's hand is up, threatening, but Mrs. Ayslin is broken already, her glasses knocked to the ground. Roughly, he grabs her thin wrist and pulls, as if to snap her in two. Egg can see Martin coming up from beside the parking lot wall but all the scaredy sweat has run out of her. Her tongue clings to the roof of her mouth and her chest itches but Egg runs between the cars and darts in front of Mr. Ayslin. He towers above her, the smell of musk, all bully beef and ham-fisted. Egg points her finger at him and shouts, "Bad dog, bad dog! Go pick on someone your own size!"

Mr. Ayslin looks surprised, that's for sure.

Mrs. Ayslin blinks, her mouth a silent *O*. She blinks as if the light is too bright, a sudden dazzle, like the wind barrelling down the foothills and Rockies, like the flash of spider thunder crackling up the dark summer sky.

She closes her mouth.

"I'll take you in, Egg," Mrs. Ayslin says.

And so Mrs. Ayslin takes Egg inside for cookies, her hand gripping too hard on Egg's shoulder but Egg doesn't mind. Chocolate chip cookies and a glass of milk too and there's no way Martin can catch her now.

Egg tells Mrs. Ayslin of the blue whales, their mysterious migration, of bumblebee bats in the jungles of Thailand. The biggest mammal and the smallest mammal, they all fit in the world. It's in the *National Geographic*. Egg tells her so.

March

It is the ultimate double bill: *Earthquake* and *The Towering Inferno*, playing for a limited engagement, and Egg can barely stand it. Chinook Ridge, squatting at the tail end of Calgary, is a beacon for all the southern towns, two strip malls that were slapped together, united under aluminum. But Chinook Ridge has a bowling alley at one end and the cinema at the other, along with Sears, Zellers, and $1.49 day Woodward's. The food court is new, along with the office tower. Chinook Ridge and everyone comes to the March Break double bill, ever since anyone can remember.

Egg rides in with Kathy, bouncing on the edge of the front seat, humming along with bands like Electric Light Orchestra and Bachman Turner Overdrive. She knows that three is a magical number. She taps her feet, squirming with excitement. Winter crisp, the snapping freeze after a lulling Chinook. Kathy is cautious at the wheel but Egg doesn't have a care. Last year at the Chinook Ridge she saw the world upside down in *The Poseidon Adventure* and she survived it. Rattling in the rusted truck, Egg sees the barren fields fall away to the first dribbles of strip malls and gas stations as they ride up Highway Two. She can see the Chinook marquee:

Now Playing
Earthquake and *The Towering Inferno*
The Shake and Bake Combo!

At the cinema Egg steps under the canopy of glittering lights and slaps down her fifty cents at the counter. Even sourpuss Kathy has to smile. They walk through the double-mirrored hall. The foyer is cavernous, enveloped by flowing curtains and faded posters of *Cat People* and *I Walked with a Zombie*. Giant kettles disgorge eruptions of popcorn and there is a gallon of soda pop bigger than her head! Milk Duds! Wigwags! Twizzlers! The pings and whistles of pinball machines! But Egg rushes forward, up the stairs, then down the hall, this maze of tunnels, the release of vaulted ceilings, the dizzying curve of the spiral staircase. Egg tugs Kathy's hand, pulling her over the threshold, into the theatre. At the front, there are big box speakers for the Sensurround effects. They scramble into their seats ("Not too close to the screen," Kathy says), Egg bouncing on her springy cushion just as the lights fade, the curtains open and—hush—down into the dark.

. . .

The lights come up and Kathy isn't beside her. Egg goes through the stuttering lights, the clatter and clang of the hall. She catches the whiff of stale buttered popcorn, that edge of rancid sweetness. Too many people and Egg is lost, it's all elbows and stomachs with big brass buckles and Egg pushed to the wall because she can't even stop. Finally Egg edges through to the doors and opens them with a heave.

The last light of the day glows in a torrent of red behind a band of low-lying clouds.

The parking lot is so big and all the cars look the same.

Egg runs to the side of the building.

Kathy stands in the middle of the parking lot, the light pole beside her. The snow is falling gently, giving the air a hush, a stillness that muffles the city sounds—the cars on MacLeod, the chatter of people leaving the mall. Egg can see the sign on the pole, the letter *M*, almost floating in the play of shadows, the swirl of snowflakes as they burst from the heavy grey of dusk into the halo of light.

Kathy is surrounded by Jonathan Heap, Doug Fisken, and some boy Egg doesn't know. Pet and Stacey stand outside the circle.

Kathy is trying to talk to Stacey, but everyone is in the way, like some kind of Red Rover Red Rover I call Kathy over, except this is not a game. The air prickles Egg's skin. Her chest tightens.

Egg doesn't know what's happening but it's a mess. The boys are all around Kathy now, and Pet is stepping in front of Stacey. Why is snotty-nosed Petunia acting like she has to protect Stacey? Kathy would never hurt Stacey. The world is upside down. Stacey cries, her face crumbled like an old piece of newspaper. The air is cold and heavy and the boys are puffed up big and their words are nasty. Doug pushes Kathy and Egg knows she'll push back and then it'll be bad because she never backs down.

Time stretches, like an elastic just ready to snap.

"Kathy, I want some jujubes, do you have any money for jujubes?" Egg bursts into the circle and everybody's all around her.

It is so quiet.

Egg looks around, to their faces, and she can see their surprise. She is so small and in the middle. She says to the boy she doesn't know, "You got a jacket just like Evel Knievel. Do you know Evel Knievel? He tried to jump the Snake River Canyon. He would have made it too, but his parachute came out early, he would have."

The light is so brittle and the quiet is unsettling. The stillness stretches, straining.

Jonathan shuffles, coughs into his hand. "Come on, let's get going."

Doug Fisken leans, over Egg toward Kathy. "Fucking dyke," he spits through his teeth. His eyes glint with ice as he struts away.

Egg lets out her breath, feels the mist against her lips, her nose.

Kathy picks up Egg. She squeezes too hard and she doesn't let Egg go until they get to the truck. Kathy's shaking but Egg knows not to say anything. They drive out of Calgary, taking the Mill Road to the Badlands, past the hoodoos and the flat plain drop. On the radio Ground Control is calling Major Tom as the moon drifts over the prairie but Egg is thinking of the Rocket Man, burning up his fuel up there alone.

. . .

That night, out of her window, Egg looks over the long grass edged with frost. Brilliant in the moonlight, the blades are a crisp silver, sparkling like a field of perfect daggers. The crystalline pattern on her window makes her think of mountains and the Yeti, all alone in the Himalayas. Egg would like to know what makes the Yeti abominable. It's hairy but then all mammals are hairy. Except for dolphins. And whales. And manatees. Manatees are gentle; they are the cows of the aquatic world. Floating cows. Not everyone knows that dolphins and whales and manatees are mammals.

The Yeti and the Abominable Snowman are the same thing but just different names. Abominations are serious things.

In the Bible there is no extinction, only smoting and stoning. Mrs. MacDonnell is strangely silent on the subject of dinosaurs. She says that God is all things but then if that is true that means God is evil too. Kathy does not believe in God. Kathy will not go to Heaven. Mrs. MacDonnell says that only those who have accepted Jesus in their hearts will be allowed entrance into the Kingdom of Heaven. There are gates and everything.

Egg wonders about that. She wonders about the cicadas in her *Young Reader's Guide to Science*, the seventeen years burrowing in the dark, the cicadas, who were once mortals who became so enraptured that they sang until their bodies withered away, becoming what they loved—a song. You see, if you love it enough, it will happen. All you need is love.

She thinks of Raymond, of Leviticus and Romans. It gets all mixed up in her head, abdominal abominable and sasquatch Saskatchewan, all jumbled together like Indians and India. She knows that the world must make sense, that there's a reason to it. Mrs. MacDonnell talks of God's great plan. Egg wants to believe but she is not so sure anymore.

She thinks of that one time, at the drive-in, not *Wizard of Oz*, but before, when Egg was little, dressed in her pjs, bundled in the car for *Where the Red Fern Grows*. Mama and Papa in the front, and Kathy, Albert, and Egg in the back. Egg fell asleep before the end of the movie. She never did learn what happened to Billy and his two dogs.

The Moral of the Story, Egg thinks. Do lives have a moral? Or is it just an accident on the railway trestle over the slow flowing river?

Stacey is gone too. Is there a moral to that?

She pads to Kathy's room in her slippery socks and opens the door a peek. The hall light slices into the darkness of Kathy's room, over a corner of the bed, to the desk.

The picture of Noel MacDonald, ripped in two, lies on the floor. Kathy's books are flung into the corners, strewn on the floor. Half of the map of the world has been torn. A pin holds a corner—not land but sea. The Siberian Sea. Egg didn't know that there was a Siberian Sea.

"Kathy?"

The room is empty. Egg thinks of Raymond, chased off by Doug Fisken and his beer bottles on Main Street. Everybody knows and nobody says anything.

Moral is the meaning. The story tells you what is good and what is evil.

But Raymond, what harm did he ever do?

The night shadows dance across the ceiling as the wind howls the moon across the sky.

· · ·

Egg lies in the field behind the barn, her snow pants bunching on her calves. Her legs stick straight up in the air, her body forming the letter *L*. Her hips are solid against the earth and she holds the claw bone in her hand, scratching at the snow.

It's the flying ones she loves: Bellerophon, or Icarus who flew too close to the sun. Perseus, with his winged sandals of gold but what wrong did Medusa do?

It's the uglies, Egg thinks, everyone hates the uglies.

She tries to blow her breath into a cloud but the air is mild, a snow-blindingly bright day. She unzips the front of her jacket.

Kathy walks up beside her. She looks up to the sky. Egg can see the bags under her sister's eyes, the slump of her shoulders.

"Your pants are going to get soaked through," Kathy says grudgingly.

"They'll dry."

Kathy nods. She lies down beside her. "What are you doing?" she asks.

"Holding up the sky."

"Heavy work?"

"It's air, silly."

Kathy can't find fault with that so she lifts her legs up as well. Not a cloud.

Egg turns to her. "Is it true if you swallow chewing gum, does it get stuck in your butt and you explode?"

"Nah."

"Martin says tapioca is full of boogers."

"Martin's full of boogers."

Hawk. Or kestrel.

Egg curls up to her. "I got fifty-seven dollars in my piggy bank. You can have it."

Kathy looks at her.

"Just so you know."

"Thanks, Egg."

"Could you tell me that story again, about the girl with the little wings on her feet—"

"On her ankles—"

"She tried to cut them off with nail clippers but they grew back, they kept on growing back."

"Yeah."

"And they came back on her shoulders, and she had to wrap them up, pin them down because when the wind blew they'd puff up like an umbrella an' she'd fall over."

"They were like bat's wings, so she had to hide them."

"But they were wings, Kathy."

"They were ugly."

"I'd want wings even if they were ugly."

Kathy gives her a look, as if to say, *of course you would*. She reaches out and ruffles Egg's hair. "Come on, you sack-a-potatoes." She kicks off her shoes and lifts Egg onto her legs, an old game of airplane. Egg balances her belly on Kathy's feet and her arms stretch out against the endless blue.

"Pegasus!" Egg shouts.

"Falkor!" Kathy adds.

They laugh as the Chinook wind stirs up the early spring sky in Bittercreek, Alberta.

April

Mrs. Syms is grumpy because she is the lunch monitor now. Mrs. Ayslin is gone. She left Bittercreek and all her classes too. Egg overhears Mrs. Syms tell Vice Principal Geary that Mr. Ayslin is wearing a groove on a seat in Ol' Jake's Saloon and sucking soup out of all the cans in Gustaffson's General Store.

Egg hopes he chokes on peas.

At recess Egg takes the long way around. Then she sees Kathy's locker. Someone has scrawled *jap dyke* in black marker that you can't get off.

Egg is afraid. Because Kathy is Popular, she's on the basketball team and there are even pictures of her in the yearbook. The world does not make any sense. Albert is dead, Mama is drunk, and they are the only Japanese-Canadian family on the prairie. This is not fair and fair is fair, that's what everyone says. And now Leviticus and Romans are against them. All the world's a jumble and Egg can't tell up from down.

At home, Egg sorts through the cupboard with the old ribbons and Christmas wrapping. She is looking for a shoebox to bury her Evel Knievel. Since his adventures on the railway track, Evel Knievel is half the man he used to be. He's had his trials and tribulations. Egg is sure it has made him better than he was. That is the point of suffering, isn't it?

But what if that isn't it?

What if there isn't a Moral, or a Meaning? What if Reverend Samuels is just another bully boy? What would he say about Raymond's penguin walk?

What if God can't do anything?

And what would He say about Kathy and Stacey?

No no no.

There is a plan and things will be perfect. There is a destiny. Good things come to those who wait.

If all of it's a lie, then there is nothing. No. So many people can't be wrong.

When she steps back, she knocks over the empty whiskey bottle. She freezes and listens for a sound from Mama's room but no, Mama has not heard the thunk. As Egg places the bottle at the back of the cupboard, she sees the camera, tucked into the dark corner, almost hidden by the bag of tinsel. Gently, she pulls it up by the strap, holds it, feels the heft. She peers through the viewfinder, the little box that gives perspective.

Another clue from Albert.

. . .

Egg bursts off the porch, into the air. For a moment she eludes gravity as her arms reach out like hawk's wings catching the late evening light. The sky is stretched thin, streaks of gold, streams of blue. The days draw longer now, a burst of yellow and orange buffalo beans break the muted earth behind the barn, though the slough is still capped with rubber ice (slide across and don't break through!) and the melt trickles into the ditches alongside the road. Magpies strut on the matted straw mound by the barn, pecking at who-knows-what. Egg takes a running leap over the steps to the ground as budding stems of grass, stiff with frost, salute her. The field is a sea of purple crocuses. Her toe catches on a tuft without give and she plants headfirst into the grass.

Snow eyelashes.

But Egg bounces back and she's off.

She checks her pocket: finders keepers. She takes out the camera, loops the strap around her neck. She runs to the barn and spins.

The camera swings on the strap and the weight pulls her wider. The sky tilts and she stops, her hand cradling the camera. Careful, she tells herself, as she scuttles up the ladder, across the side shed top, to the flat roof before the crawl space window. On the flat roof she turns and pauses before the width and breadth of her domain. She feels the weight of the camera in her hands, the pull of the strap against her neck. *Click click, click click*. She likes pressing the button and pulling the lever for advancing the film, that *whirl-click* sound — that is the best.

From the side roof she can see the distant Rockies, how the jagged mountain edge recedes and contracts, like a slumbering dragon caught in perpetual dreamtime. West to the foothills, the land of the giant vole-moles, with their starfish noses and ferocious claws.

Egg hisses at the air and claws, most vole-like.

"Egg!"

She starts, almost tumbles.

It is Kathy, calling from below. "Goddamnit Egg, you're gonna break your neck!"

Egg's arms fall to her sides. She watches Kathy get into the truck. The tires kick up gravel as Kathy pulls up and away. Kathy Grumpycakes Moodymug Murakami. Kathy, with her own secret life. Sometimes it seems like Kathy is trying to wriggle out of her own skin. Egg's heart lurches as she gazes at her sister, the fishtail of the truck pulling out of the drive. She feels protective and so she throws out her arms for an *abracadabra*. Do abominations get blessings? There must be another word for that.

She ducks into the loft, her crawl space, into her secret niche above the pens. She blinks away the dust, her eyes growing used to the dark (always so dark in the ostrich barn) and glances past her clutter and her comic books.

She stops.

The ostriches are inside but there is no scratching, no chirps, no calls, only a strange kind of rasping. Egg feels the cold creep up her arms, like a draft. She freezes — that sound again, like something strangled. She stoops and peers through the eye-knot in the floor.

Her father draws the hush around him.

Egg feels the clutch in her lungs.

Beside him lies an ostrich, so still, too still. The bulk of feathers is a stark contrast to the bare thin flesh of the legs. It seems so wrong, those legs, stick-skinny and broken, like a toy smashed up and thrown away. Her father's breath is harsh in such quiet, and Egg can see the ostrich, the limp, fragile neck and clouded liquid eyes. Goose pimples. Egg wants to pull away, out of the loft but her legs are so heavy, knees so weak, she's pressed down to the floor. She thinks of the frozen figures of Pompeii, the petrified stumps outside the Badlands, Lot's wife and all of Jericho trumpets blasting; did they kill the children too?

Her father is so still. Fumbling, Egg makes it to the ladder, down to the boxes. She stands by the chick pen. She is afraid to come closer.

"Papa," Egg says. It is like dropping a stone down a chasm.

Her father does not turn. He kneels by the broken body, his hand stroking the feathered wing. He says, "Dog got in last night. Dog or coyote. Little bit of panic inside. This one got her head caught up in the bars. Snapped her neck." Her father speaks in a voice so rough, as if torn out of a too-small space and caught on the jagged edges, twisting and pulling away.

"They're stupid creatures. Jittery. They're strong and fast, but they're skittish. Gets them into trouble. She only had to pull her head up..."

He blinks, as if trying to make sense of it. He stares. He is lost in his own vision of the bars, the broken neck.

The elephants, Egg thinks. She gazes at his unruly hair, the wiry strength of his frame. She wants to help him, her Papa, but she is afraid.

He stands. "Go. Just go, Egg."

She starts forward but he swings back, his hand raised, dismissive. His knuckles meet her chin, the click of her teeth knocking together, the shock of contact.

Egg falls back.

The shadows of the barn weave in and out, the bars and beams and the darkness of the loft. The ostriches shudder, their plume, a quivering dance, their long legs scratch at the straw in the pens, their necks bob and peck, a jerking motion. The ostriches scratch and flare, kicking at the barn gate, hissing at the bars.

Papa stands, frozen.

Egg feels the straw and grit beneath the palm of her hand, a numbness in her jaw. She runs, her hair clinging to the dampness of her forehead as she races to the house.

In her room she stomps on the Lego and dinky cars. Crash crash crash. It doesn't matter anyway. Let it all fall down.

. . .

Her pictures are back, the film from Albert's camera taken into Gustafsson's General Store, sent on to Calgary, and now, in Egg's hands, this tidy little package. She crawls beneath her bed and opens the flap of the envelope.

Egg likes packages.

In the first few shots of the barn, the ostriches are fuzzy, feathery lumps, and here, what looks to be Egg's thumb encroaching on the viewfinder. Behind the barn, the blank field races to the horizon. Egg has started reading about photography. In the *Young Reader's Guide to Science*, there is a glass triangle that holds all the colour. If you shine a beam of light, the colours can all come out — *presto magico*! Egg thinks it would be neat if you could shine a light on people and all their stuff came out — all the happy and sad — like X-ray vision.

Egg would like a superpower. Just one.

Egg thinks her photographs are nice but things are more real in real life. In photographs everything looks far away. Sometimes it doesn't even look like now. She peers closely at the photo of the barn, at the shadows of the wall. Her finger rubs a streak, a smudge; it looks like there's a face—Albert's face. She drops the envelope and goes screaming to Kathy.

Kathy takes a look at Egg's pictures, at the ghosties in the dark wall of the barn. Then she clucks her tongue and says, "Double exposure."

Egg bounces on one foot. "Are you sure? Albert's not stuck in the camera, is he?"

"No. It's old film. See, someone took a picture and you just took a picture on top of it, so that's why it looks like that. Besides, there's no such thing as ghosts."

Kathy, who has an empirical method and everything.

Egg runs to her bedroom and slides under her bed. Her magnifying glass is there. She checks the darker objects in the photos, a bush, the side shed, the blackness of the slough. She shuffles through the photographs, searching—shadows are the key. Nekoneko on the drawer, the sparkle of the china bureau, the stubble field that retreats to the horizon. The last picture is of the barn in twilight. In that print, she sees it, an image; she can barely make it out. Her hand trembles; it is Evangeline.

. . .

Kathy finally relents and takes Egg into town for the grocery run. But Egg has other plans. With her magnifying glass snug in her pocket, she is on her own mission. There's a mystery here, hidden in the photographs, the ghost images. It is like an Encyclopedia Brown Choose Your Own Adventure. They drive past the Dairy Dream, the rundown grounds of the old stockyard and park by Robertson's Repair-All. Egg doesn't say that there is a parking space in front of Heap's Hardware, even if it is closer to Gustafsson's General Store. The storefront of

Robertson's Repair-All is chock full of ancient televisions and radios. The light beams out of a dusty box against the glare of the afternoon sun.

Kathy hands her the empty cardboard box, pulled from the back of the truck. "Here, you take this in. I'll just be a second."

Egg shuffles to the store, the bell on the door jangling loudly. All heads turn, voices drop. Egg shrinks. It's like stumbling into a room where she does not belong, when *Japanese* turns into *Jap*. Mrs. Crawley is there, with five of her sewing circle, their heads all tucked together. By the counter, Mrs. Gustafsson, her voice too proud to fall, says, "Not that one. It's the sister."

Egg feels like something under a microscope. She backs into the door, only to have it swing open. She almost bumps into Kathy.

"What is it?" Kathy asks.

Kathy has not heard the voices.

"Nothing." Egg places the cardboard box on the counter and scoots away.

Egg skulks by the doorway as Kathy asks for her stack of newspapers. The long aisles of Gustafsson's are packed with canned meats, sacks of sugar, salt, and flour, and short, long, thick, thin sausages dangle behind the counter. Peach baskets line the floor, filled with apples and onions. There is a briny pickle barrel near the door. On the counter, in a glass display, sits a tray of pastries, swirls of cinnamon and marzipan. The cash register still has the old sign of Gustafsson's Supplies. Mrs. Gustafsson stands behind the till, her smile so tight. Egg thinks, you couldn't squeeze a penny from her. On the counter, she can see *The Globe and Mail's War in Review*, a picture of a burning man. She can see the outline of his robes, the shaven head, serene repose. She picks out a word: immolation.

This is not what she came for.

"Kathy," she says, "I'm going to wait outside."

Kathy, fingers drumming on the cardboard box at the counter, nods absently.

Egg steps out the door. She looks down the street, to the intersection of Main and Maple.

Evangeline lives two blocks down in a bird box house, the asphalt siding peeling from the corners. The rose bushes are all twisted vines and prickles, weaving into the iron fence that surrounds the sagging porch. Egg thinks, Rapunzel. The windows are closed, curtains drawn. This is worse than a tower with no stairs and no doors.

Egg presses the bell.

Evangeline Granger opens the door, wisps of hair tucked behind her ears, curled at the nape of her neck, as the notes of "Sola, Perduta, Abbandonata" float through the air. At the sight of Egg, Evangeline does not move, there is no surprise, as if she has been expecting Egg all along. There are dark circles under her beautiful eyes. Evangeline Granger holds time in the creases of her lips, in the pinch of her brow. Someone must release her.

Egg places the photographs in front of her. Evangeline does not look at them but she reaches out and her hand strokes back Egg's hair and she says:

"I would have liked to have had a child. She would have been like you."

Then Egg knows. Evangeline loved him. She feels it, a burst of exhilaration, a discovery like the flare of a match strike, and then a plummeting realization: Evangeline, who has been kind to Egg, all for his sake. Not for her at all.

"Why did he die?"

There are ordinary things in ordinary life: a cup, a chair, a favourite sweater. There is the dark side of the moon that knows no light. Evangeline's eyes are like that—a door that opens and closes.

"I don't know, Egg. Sometimes you just don't know. Not even grown-ups."

"He fell. They said he fell."

Evangeline stands so still, dawn-lake still, reflecting the morning light. "I used to love it here. I used to think that it was the best place on earth, the sky so big, everything so clear. You could see a storm coming from miles away. That's what I thought." Evangeline's voice is so soft, as if Egg is not even there. "We were driving out of town. Well, we were running away. Fresh start. I mean, we couldn't stay in Bittercreek, not with me and...well. We made it past Four Corners when I saw my father chasing us. So we took the Mill Road to the trestle. We saw the train coming down, thought we could make it."

"You raced the train?" No one races the train.

"No, we stopped right in front of the crossing. My father hit us from behind, pushed us up onto the track and the train hit us. All three of us. Bumpers got hitched. Funny, eh?" But Evangeline is not laughing. "Albert got thrown. They had to pry my father from the steering wheel. And I lost the baby."

There was a baby?

Her hand strokes her belly and Egg understands.

"So Kathy lied." Egg is almost crying. "She's going to go to Hell."

"No," Evangeline shakes her head. "Oh, Egg," she holds her and Egg can feel the tremor, the flutter deep inside. "No one's going to Hell." Evangeline's eyes hold the stars, as she strokes back Egg's hair. She says, "Sometimes it isn't about good and evil, it's about good and good. We try the best we can. And we try to make that enough."

. . .

With one last glance at Evangeline, Egg closes the door behind her.

Superman works alone. He has a cape and everything. His only weakness is kryptonite, from his home planet of Krypton. Superman, exiled, saved from his dying world by his mother and father, who loved him, loved him more than anything, loved him and sacrificed themselves so that he could be saved. Egg puzzles this over. What does it mean when your greatest vulnerability comes from those you love the best? His fortress is called Solitude. The strongest man alive and he is still lonely.

Egg thinks Rumpelstiltskin wanted to be found. It must be lonely sometimes, spinning straw into gold, in the middle of a dark forest. He didn't want to hide anymore. She thinks he just wanted a family and maybe if someone knew him by his one true name, they would love him. It's like hide-and-seek and you wait and wait and if no one comes, that is sad. If someone comes, your stomach squishes, and then—ta-da!—what a relief! But if you hide and hide and then finally someone sees you as you really are and they don't love you, that is the worst thing. That is the worst.

Egg sits on the curb and twists her shoelaces. Now she has evidence of Albert, the mystery of her older, bigger brother. She has evidence but in the beginning the question was different, the mystery isn't the same. Claudia Kincaid solved the puzzle in the *Mixed-Up Files* and she became Changed but Egg's all a muddle in her brain.

Was it all wrong? Maybe Albert never had any answers anyway.

The Moral of the Story:

Evangeline loved Albert but she couldn't save him. What's the point of love if you can't save anyone? What's the point of anything?

Maybe it's a trick from the very beginning, a game that you can never win, like the carnival prizes down at the Stampede.

Nothing changes. Newton tells you that.

Egg rambles down Main, her foot kicking a fist-sized rock down the street. With one great jump-kick, she knocks the stone off the side of Nelson's Barber Shop, a ricochet down Maple. She thinks of the burning man on *The Globe and Mail*. She thinks of Newton, his equal and opposites. Maybe good and evil are like that. Maybe there is a balance to the universe and it all works out in the end.

"Get her!"

Egg nearly jumps out of her skin at the sight of Glenda, Chuckie, and Martin Fisken. She tears off, down between the brick-tar-sheet houses, scrambling through the fences, a long scratch from the wire. Her heart skips as Fiskens' dog bursts from out of nowhere, as it chases her down the length of the fence. She ducks through the backyard, a cacophony of shouts and squeals, through the maze of sheets hanging from the Geary clothesline, the sting in her eyes and panic's stitch in her side.

Run run run over the garden patch, the green crunch as she crashes through the string and wire, down through the alley by the hardware fence.

The gate, though, is locked.

The voices shrill behind her.

Egg throws herself high, toes digging into the mesh, arms hauling up, the swing of the fence takes her weight, but higher, she scrambles higher, lifts herself, leaning over the bar, almost there—

They grab her ankle, pull her down, pull her back, the wire cutting into her gut, even as she kick kick kicks, there are too many hands—then down, thrown down to the ground.

Egg blinks through her tears.

Glenda, Chuckie, and Martin Fisken.

They hold a gopher, speared through the eye. Jelly glaze. But it moves. Egg can see that the gopher is covered with maggots and it moves.

That's when she begins to scream.

. . .

Egg blinks. There is a red dot in the sky. No, a yellow spot. If she closes her eyes, the red dot takes its place.

If she closes her eyes, the world goes away.

Slowly she sits up and holds out her arms, the raised welts, her bloodied scratches. Her skin is on fire. She thinks of the well and closes her eyes.

The dark. The welcoming dark.

I've killed the sun.

. . .

Mrs. Syms walks by Egg's desk and peers at her sheet of abc's. The lesson is penmanship and Mrs. Syms frowns at Egg's chicken scratches. At the corner of the page, she sees Egg's drawing and looks at Egg as if she has sprouted wings. "It's a sphinx," Egg explains, "from the Greek myths."

"My God," she shudders. "What have you been reading? The Greeks!" Mrs. Syms shivers, "who eat their children and marry their mothers!"

She glares at her, as if she's killed Baby Jesus.

Mrs. Syms believes. But in a hard, cold way that hates everything around her. It's like she wants the cross, the crown of thorns, wants it more than love. Her love is God's avenging sword.

Mrs. Syms sits at her desk, rattling her pencils. "Children," she says, "let's begin the last chapter of *Charlotte's Web.*"

Egg picks up her book and wiggles with delight. This is her favourite part of the story, where Charlotte is finally seen, after all the toil and trouble, Charlotte finally gets her reward.

Mrs. Syms begins reading, recounting Wilbur's triumph and salvation before the Judges, but as she reads on, Egg shifts. This is not how the story goes. The words tumble from Mrs. Syms's mouth, lies of how sickly Charlotte becomes, and finally how she dies, so alone in the empty fairgrounds.

Egg sits rigid in her chair. She knows the story. Charlotte doesn't die. Kathy has told her. Kathy wouldn't lie. It's a story and you can't change the end of a story. That's where the moral is. Good things come to those who wait. The righteous are victorious. The little engine that could.

Mrs. Syms closes the book, a murderer with a smile on her face.

Egg is burning Hellfire.

"No."

Mrs. Syms looks up in surprise. "Egg—"

Egg stands on her chair, finger pointing at Mrs. Syms. "No, no, no! Liar, liar!" Egg is screaming, the words spewing out of her, like poison. She doesn't know what she says, doesn't care as she grabs her Anne Frank from the desk and runs to the library because the library has all the answers, because the dictionary says what is what and the words will never lie. Egg slides into the lowest shelf and pulls the book cart in front of her. Anne Frank will tell her. Egg knows that endings are important.

She flips to the back of the book, the part that she has never read, the part that Kathy tells her at bedtime. She reads that Anne Frank died in Bergen-Belsen concentration camp. That she never went to America, that she isn't singing on Broadway, that she will never be the actress that she always wanted to be. Egg knows then that Kathy lies, that perversion means upside down and that Kathy is a pervert of lies and lies. How many lies does it take to make a liar? Egg's eyes burn, tears stream down her cheeks. The world cannot be like this. Egg rushes to the history shelves and scans the volumes, the heavy, ponderous tomes. The shelf of World War II. She tumbles the books into the aisle, the pages opening to maps, to black and white photographs. *The Yellow Star* falls open to a map of extermination and concentration camps. She reads about death, the Final Solution. The words jumble and betray. Not even the Dictionary can make sense of this world. There is something horrifically scientific about it. Zyklon B. What would Newton say about this? And God? Death in a railcar. Death in a shallow pit. Death, so naked and so alone. Charlotte. Anne. Cold death burnt to ashes.

Bad things happen and you cannot help it. Bad things happen and there is no why.

Egg stares at the photograph on the back of the *Diary of a Young Girl*, gazes into the luminous eyes of the young girl, hands clasped before her. No, there are no more books from Anne Frank. There will be no more. "I'm sorry," Egg sobs. "I'm sorry."

She runs out of the library, down the hall, but Mrs. Syms's raven's claws reach out for her and it is down down down the long echoing hall to the Principal's office for her.

. . .

Mrs. Jonas, the secretary, attacks the typewriter *clacketty clack* like she is playing Beethoven. Mrs. Jonas pops pink baby aspirins like she's popping chicklets. She calls her makeup "war paint" and she has the lipstick to prove it. As Egg sits outside Principal Crawley's office, Egg watches Mrs. Jonas carefully. Clacketty clack don't look back and zing of the carriage return. Mrs. Jonas has all her fingers going at once. There is a whole symphony there, the words beneath the music. Egg wonders about Miss Granger and the music she hears inside. Miss Granger would never call lipstick "war paint."

Inside Principal Crawley's office, they are meeting, Kathy and Crawley. To See What Is To Be Done. Egg swings her legs, trying not to think about it. She can't quite reach the ground.

The door opens and Kathy steps out. Her mouth is as flat as a roadkill gopher — three days baked and pancaked by a semi.

Egg closes her eyes. Clacketty clack, don't look back.

Kathy sits down beside her.

"You think I'm stupid," Egg blurts.

"No, no," but Kathy's head barely moves.

"Anne Frank, she wrote the book, I saw her picture. You told me, you told me she's working in the Empire State Building."

Kathy opens her mouth. No words.

Egg storms, "You told me Charlotte and Wilbur go to Las Vegas. You told me! But now everybody's dead. They die and they die and it doesn't help anything." Egg's chest heaves. Her breath comes bigger, as if she's spilling over. "You shouldn't lie to me, Kathy. I've been practising for weeks now."

"Practising?" Kathy looks puzzled.

"The march to Auschwitz."

Kathy stares at her.

"If you survive the worst things, nothing bad could ever happen. Not anymore."

"Egg."

Egg hears the flatness in Kathy's voice. Dead flat, gopher flat. Mama flat. "And with your scholarship—"

"There isn't any scholarship. Not for me."

Egg bites her lip. But Kathy has to leave Bittercreek. A small voice inside her whispers, *she's staying for you, because you're useless, because you're weak.* "I would have survived. I would have made it. Don't you think, Kathy? Don't you think it's a terrible way to die?"

"Yes, Egg. It's a terrible way to die."

Kathy shuffles to her feet. "C'mon."

"Albert told me ostriches don't fly."

"Ostriches don't fly."

"Is he in Heaven?"

Kathy lifts her head but she can't say the words. She's frozen, like Papa—frozen, like Mama with her whiskey. Egg's fists ball up and she is hitting Kathy but they bounce off like Kathy's turned to stone. Egg is crying, shouting, and she doesn't care who sees. "Liar! Liar! You lie about everything! I hate you, I hate you, I HATE YOU!" Egg screams and then she runs.

By the school bus she gasps, clutching the steel mesh fence. She can feel the evil cling to her. The ink blots spreading, the stain, her soul is staining. Mrs. MacDonnell knows that she is the dirty one, the uglies have got her. The words are wrong, the day is wrong and Anne, she is lost among the thousand million miles between time and time again. *Diaphanous.* But you can't be invisible with this stain. The words slip away, away from her, they run away from ugly. The Dictionary cannot save her.

. . .

She takes her Callard's candy tin from behind the shelf in the library and runs to Evangeline Granger's house. She leaves it on the step with the envelope of pictures. Egg would have left One-Eyed Nekoneko with her but Kathy should have that. Someone to look out for her. Anne Frank she will take to the end.

. . .

In her secret room above the ostriches, Egg places Big Jim and Evel Knievel in front of her. Big Jim with his melted karate chop and the many pieces of Evel Knievel. Smoted, just like that. Job in the Bible, he was a righteous man but God and the Devil got in the way. God and the Devil are like opposites but not.

Anne Frank is dead, Charlotte the spider is dead, and Albert is dead. Dead dead dead. Anne Frank in America is a made-up fake story. Lies are bad and Kathy lied.

But that isn't right. Kathy tried to protect her but who will protect Kathy? Leviticus and the Romans scream from the pulpit and all of Bittercreek too.

Kathy can't stay here and Egg is making her stay. There are things Egg can do.

Egg can make herself invisible. It is as close to a superhero as she can get.

She crawls out to the side shed roof and makes her way down, her comics and Anne Frank tucked under her arm.

She has a plan.

The wind has fallen and Egg feels the heat lifting from the earth. Dust curdles in the lines of her palms and the back of her neck itches. Across the horizon, the sky is a stone blue, a blanket that tucks in the dark. Good night, good night, Egg says.

Good night.

In their pens the ostriches sit, a clump of feathers, on their scratched-out ground nests.

Egg opens the gate of each of the pens. Two of the ostriches run into the dark. Three of them sit, listless. One runs in a circle.

Stupid birds.

Egg goes right to the gate of the barn and opens it and tells her Papa that the ostriches are loose and out he goes. Easy peasy.

Egg goes to the back wall, where Albert's things are stored, and opens the suitcase and puts her comics inside.

She holds Anne Frank to her chest.

She takes the matches. Strike and flare. The comics curl and blacken with red hot edges. She throws the notebook on the pile as the embers hiss, darting upwards. There are no answers. There is no sense to it; her scribbles did not change anything. Her stupid story of the Japanese-Canadian family on the ostrich farm will come to ashes. It does not matter. The world will burn. Let it take all the pain, all the grief. Let it end for there is nothing more. Albert is dead, there is no Heaven for him, and everyone lies. Egg steps back as the suitcase bursts into flame, sparks leaping into the air.

The fire lives and breathes, choking her, the heat like the surface of the sun. It hurts. She climbs up to the crawl space, the smoke curling black and thick. Egg sits, tucking in her legs. She sees the beams in the far wall blacken, a seam of seething red. She hears the crackle of flame.

The burning man. A sacrifice. So Kathy can be free.

Egg thinks of one-eyed Kitty and the Callard's toffee tin and Superman with his Fortress of Solitude. Cotton-cloud candy and Dalmatian Blue who always says "Safety first." She thinks of the burning monk, the girl on the napalm road, and Anne, wings spread, angel-feathered.

Fire. Albert was right after all. The flames of the Ouiji were the answer.

If she dies, she'll take the uglies with her, the black spots melting in the uplifting air. She will fall into the well and it will be over with. It will be nothing, at last.

. . .

Through the hiss and the roar of the conflagration, Egg hears Kathy calling her name. The embers fly upward like a buzzing horde and the fire, the ripple waves of heat, how the flames claw up the planks like some living, writhing creature.

Egg stares at the devouring shades of orange, the bright flash flare as the beams groan and shudder. Her eyes burn as she draws herself tighter, the air blisters, and it's like her skin is being torn away.

"Egg!"

Kathy is there, by the side slant roof, the ladder holding her, but the roof, eaten away by the flames—she cannot come any closer.

"Egg!" Kathy screams.

No no no, this is not part of the plan. Egg sees Kathy, as she tries to climb onto the side roof, that burst of flame as her arm breaks through the wood, a wince and fumble as Kathy hangs onto the ladder.

Kathy looks afraid.

And then Egg knows. Kathy, she will try, she will die trying, always to save her. She will make herself weak so that Egg can be strong.

Kathy would do that for her. Because she loves her.

Kathy reaches, arms stretched out. "Help me, Goddamnit!"

It's not fair, this life, the meanness, the daily tests that we cannot help but fail. The flames cackle, a mocking howl as Egg whimpers. No, she cannot do it, she cannot be strong.

The flames whip around her. The whirlwind.

But Egg.
She can be Egg.

She rises. She can feel the scorching heat, the oily soot-ash against her cheeks. No. She will show them. The girl with the bat's wings, she will fly, faster than the speed of light, over the hoodoos and coulees that surround Bittercreek, over the barren flat plains, over the jagged-toothed Rockies. Damn the old trestle bridge, the wars and famines, and all the disasters of Biblical proportions. Damn the beasts of Revelation, the fear and the terror of the Bittercreek gang, Leviticus and Romans too. Against the whirlwind, she will be herself. Egg runs towards the crawl space window, through the thick, blackened air, she jumps across the side shed roof into her sister's arms. Kathy grabs her in a dizzying embrace, a clashing fall as the ladder topples back, the sudden smack of cool earth, the wisp of a cool dewfall night.

Mama rushes forward, the strangled cries twisting in her throat. She clutches Egg, her grip almost hurting. Her face is streaked with tears, her eyes still wild and bewildered. She grabs Egg by the shoulders and stares into her face.

"My baby." Her Mama's eyes, shining through her tears. "My baby." Mama holds her. She will not let Egg go.

"Egg."

Mama looks up and Egg follows her gaze. Her father staggers towards them, clothes singed, his face smeared with ash. His hands go to Egg's head, stroking down her hair.

"Egg, Egg…" It is all that he can say.

. . .

Egg lies in her bed, wrapped up in her favourite blanket. She can barely keep her eyes open but the feel of Kathy's hand, stroking back her hair, is comforting—she can't quite let go. Her hair is still damp from the bath and she wonders if she will have to pee. Everyone knows that if you go to bed with a wet head, you will pee during the night. On the walls of her bedroom, Egg sees the reflected lights of the fire truck. The wheels grind against the rough stones in the drive.

The red flashes pull away.

Kathy is all shadows. She must be angry, Egg thinks. She can feel the tremor through the bed, Kathy's hand gripping the sheet.

"Why did you do it?" Kathy's voice is rough, abraded. Egg can hear her biting down at the end.

There is a strange, choking noise in the dark. Finally, Kathy says, "You can't leave me, you know. And Nekoneko, she'd be lonely."

Egg sits up. Her sister is weeping. Kathy, who never cries, who takes on all her battles, who puts up her dukes and never backs down. Kathy, who hates the weak, who would keep her secrets until the day she dies. "I'm sorry, I'm sorry," Kathy chokes.

Egg wants to tell her that there are no sorrys, it's not her fault, it's nobody's fault at all, and it hits her that maybe this could be true. "It's all right," Egg whispers and strokes back Kathy's hair. Kathy sobs, tears damp against Egg's shoulder, a body shudder that breaks down all the sadness, all the grief. Her sister loves her. And even through her tears, Egg knows that she has done something right.

May

Egg sits on the steps of the library, her bookbag beside her. She looks to the empty playground as the late afternoon sun crawls over her shoulder. Today is Kathy's basketball day. Today the scout has come all the way from the east. Kathy is inside the gym, practising with her team. Egg takes a deep breath. She must be ready just in case her big sister needs her. The bright yellow school bus for the Sand River Scorpions pulls up at the parking lot with a rattle and a whinge. Egg can tell it is the Scorpions because of the long red spider-thing stinger painted on the side of the bus. The girls scramble out of the bus, wearing their jackets of white and red. Their crest is a scorpion's tail, curved like the fancy swords in all the novels with wizards and elves and dragons. Egg is fascinated. They huddle in a circle, hunched, a low chant which builds, exploding into a "Scorpions—Sting!" with fists raised, a jumping jack. But Egg thinks that they are not so much different than the Bittercreek team. Egg checks her watch. She loves the heavy feel of the metal on her wrist. Papa's watch but she is just borrowing it.

She is going to make a sundial for her science project but this ticktock is good enough for now.

. . .

When Egg steps into the gym, the booming echo hits her like a wave, the chatter of the people in the bleachers, the high-pitched whistle of the referee. All of Bittercreek is here, along with a good chunk of Sand River for the basketball finals. Egg sees the sign — Bittercreek Eagles versus the Sand River Scorpions. Principal Crawley and Ms. Chapman sit in the first tier of seats. Vice Principal Geary staggers by the rear doors, as Coach Wagner paces the line. Where is the scout? What does a scout look like?

Egg searches the court. Her breath is high in her throat.

She sees her sister. Kathy runs down the court in that sideways stride. At the end line, she shakes out her hands, her fingers flexing. Egg calls out to her, waving her arm as high as she can. Kathy waves back, her finger pointing towards the bench. Egg takes a seat by Coach Wagner. Kathy has saved her a special place so Egg won't miss anything.

The Scorpions' captain, with the name Thornton emblazoned on the back of her uniform, walks to the side court, hands on her hips. The other team looks bigger, taller, but Kathy has told her that size is not everything. Equal and opposite may not be so equal and opposite. Egg spies someone standing by Principal Crawley's side: a small white man in a canary-yellow bow tie, his suit a herringbone grey. Could it be the scout from the east with a scholarship in his back pocket?

Tweetie Bird, she thinks.

Kathy and the Scorpion captain stand at the centre. The tipoff, Egg remembers.

Bittercreek blue and Sand River red. At the blast of the whistle, the players gather like a fist and then an open palm: clutch and then scatter. The crowd roars as the ball goes into play, back and forth, a feint, and dribble.

Egg's stomach crunches up.

A hand cups her shoulder. Egg looks up to see Evangeline smiling at her. Evangeline, in a dress of purple violets. Egg thinks of Albert. He would have loved to see his sister take on the Scorpions for the championship finals. Egg straightens her back, her throat constricting. Yes, that would have been nice. Albert is gone gone gone but Papa's back in the house, fixing up the ostrich barn with Jack Henry, and Mama has poured all the whiskey down the drain. Mama still cries but her hugs are tighter now.

Egg holds the tug at her chest. She thinks of blue whales and bumblebee bats. Heroes and dragons and Damsels Fair. She thinks of Rumpelstiltskin who wanted to be known and loved. She wants a world with Anne Frank in it.

Egg looks over the crowd. She sees Mrs. Figgis, whose brother was killed in Burma, Ms. Chapman, with her Russian novels. Martin Fisken squirms on the bench, his ear twisted by his big brother Doug. By the doors, little Jimmy Simpson bounces on his toes; his gait reminds Egg of the penguin's walk.

It makes Egg wonder how Bittercreek can be so small and so big at the same time. A kaleidoscope's twist will always surprise you. Against the universe, the Earth is a tiny speck but somewhere out there, Raymond makes his way in the world. Mrs. Ayslin, too, without her sunglasses.

A cheer ricochets from wall to wall. Kathy has just landed her first basket. Egg screams as loud as she can, "Go, Kathy go!"

Kathy beams at the crowd; she has heard Egg's call. Egg waves and Kathy catches it. She nods, giving her a thumbs-up and a smile. With the scout in the stands, she must be all butterflies but still she has a moment for her sister.

Next September, her sister will be up and away, but away is not forever.

Nothing is forever. That's what Newton says. Her notebook was lost in the fire, but she can start a new one.

The red and blue uniforms dart down the court. Sand River on the defensive! A tall player in red, the one with the long blond ponytail, bodychecks Kathy with a slam to the gut but Kathy is up before the ref can even call a foul. With two steps and a jump, the ball is back in Kathy's hands. She sprints down the court, but Egg can see the point guard on her tail. Egg wants to scream *Look out, Kathy!* but Kathy jumps, twisting slightly, her elbow tucked under the throw, releasing the ball in a snap as she shoots up and out. Egg stares at the ball turning, the arc of its orbit.

The ball spins. Egg stands on her seat.

One shot and everyone watching.

Egg holds her breath and stretches out her arms. Like bumble-bee bats. Like wings.

Acknowledgements

It is no small thing to believe in a book. I am grateful to all at Goose Lane Editions, especially my editor Bethany Gibson for her truly heroic efforts. Thanks to my family who have supported me for all these years (in Toronto and Vancouver) and my wonderful readers: Ilana Landsberg-Lewis, Terrie Hamazaki, Susan Mazza, Moni Kim, Andrea Chow, and Bo Yih Thom.

To my communities:
Tanya Thompson, Heather Hermant, Melina Young, Tina Garnett, Jennifer Marie Mason, Hiromi Goto, Nozomi Goto, Aruna Srivastava, Ashok Mathur, Sharon Proulx-Turner, the late Tiger Goto and his introduction to the Desert Wind Ranch (I learned everything about ostriches from the Rossmans—thank you!—so many years ago). To all at the Stephen Lewis Foundation for their encouragement and their own passionate work—Joanna Henry, my fellow Tater Crapauder, I am looking at you. Special thanks to Wayson Choy at the Humber School for Writers Summer Workshop, and my agent, Margaret Hart.

Linda Chen for knitting and New York.

The story of Egg originally popped up in Aritha Van Herk's Creative Writing Class at the University of Calgary—I tip my hat to my friends and colleagues.

Ilana, Zev, and Yoav, you have given me so much.

Without Bo Yih, I would not have finished this book.

I would like to thank the Canada Council, the Ontario Arts Council Writers' Reserve and Works in Progress, and the Toronto Arts Council for their financial support.

A Special Note on the Musical and Literary Accompaniment

May I humbly acknowledge the different inspirations that have contributed to *Prairie Ostrich*: Elton John's "Rocket Man," David Bowie's "Space Oddity," Cat Stevens's "Oh Very Young," and Nancy Sinatra's "Bang Bang," along with Giacomo Puccini's "Sola, Perduta, Abbandonata" and "O Mio Babbino Caro."

Books inspire books and stories are built on stories. I first read *Anne Frank: Diary of a Young Girl* when I was struggling through my adolescence. *Prairie Ostrich* owes so much to that budding writer of the Secret Annex. *Charlotte's Web* came much later in my life, but E.B. White made me love spiders. *From the Mixed-Up Files of Basil E. Frankweiler* to *A Wrinkle in Time*, I am beholden to so many novels, short stories, and poems. Thank you, all.